TIGHT ROPE

JULIE MULHERN

J & M PRESS

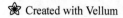

To the readers who've stuck with Ellison through body after body, thank you. You're the reason I write.

ACKNOWLEDGMENTS

Boy oh boy, does it take a village.
Thank you to Edie and Matt.
This wouldn't happen without you.

And, Joey, thanks for hanging with me!

CHAPTER ONE

August 1975
Kansas City, Missouri

A phone ringing in the middle of the night is never a good thing. Never. No one rings at two a.m. to crow about their son's promotion or confide that their daughter got engaged to that young lawyer who's making a name for himself at the firm. No one calls to share that there's a private sale at Swanson's and the dress I've been eyeing is thirty percent off.

Nope. Calls in the wee hours were harbingers of doom.

So, when a *brnng, brngg* dragged me from my dreams, and the clock on the bedside table read two-fifteen, I sat up and clutched the sheets to my chest as my husband picked up the receiver.

"Jones." His voice was calm. Even. If I'd picked up the receiver, I'd have sounded panicked, like disaster was yanking on the straps of my nightgown.

An endless moment passed as he listened to whoever was on the other end of the line. What had happened? Was his family in California, okay?

Unable to stand the suspense, I whispered, "Who is it?"

He gave a brief, apologetic wince. "Work."

I leaned back against the pillows and exhaled slowly. My husband was a homicide detective. You'd think there would be more early morning calls. But, most nights, our sleep was blessedly undisturbed. This awakening came as an unwelcome shock.

With the phone still pressed to his ear, Anarchy threw off the sheet and the summer-weight blanket and swung his feet to the floor. "I understand, sir. I'm on my way."

With my portion of the sheet still crinkled in my hands, I watched as he replaced the receiver. "Someone we know?"

"I don't think so. It sounds like a mob hit."

Worry tightened my stomach. I'd seen *The Godfather*. A mob hit meant violent men and shoot-outs and cannoli. "Your captain formed a mob task force." Anarchy had told me all about it over dinner a few weeks ago. "Shouldn't they be handling this?"

"Norris and McFarland are both on vacation. That means the task force has vice guys. They've got narcotics guys. They've even got a forensic accountant. No homicide detectives."

I forced my fingers to relax and held my tongue even though I longed to demand, *"Why you?"* Anarchy was the detective they assigned when a prominent lawyer murdered his wife, or a doctor poisoned his patients. *A mob hit. Dangerous men. A dangerous investigation.* I aggressively smoothed the now-wrinkled cotton sheet and tried to act like a supportive wife. "Let me guess, a dead guy in the trunk of a car?"

"Yep." He disappeared into the closet

I turned on the light on my bedside table and blinked at the sudden brightness. "Was the car set on fire?" When the Kansas City mob wanted to make a statement, they set their corpses on fire.

He perched on the edge of the mattress and pulled on a pair of khaki pants, then buttoned a shirt over his chest and frowned. "From what the captain said, I don't think so."

In a preemptive maneuver, I hopped out of bed. "I'll get your jacket. Do you need a tie?" Left to his own devices, my otherwise perfect husband would mix plaids.

"Yes."

I hurried into the closet, returning a moment later with a navy sports coat and one of the tasteful ties I'd bought for him at Harzfeld's.

"Thanks." He dropped a kiss on my cheek, then looped the tie around his neck.

"Where did they find the car?" That sounded so much better than asking where they found the body.

His deft fingers fumbled, and his gaze slid to the left.

"Anarchy?"

He glanced at the ceiling before finally meeting my gaze. "The parking lot at the country club."

CHAPTER TWO

I stumbled into the kitchen shortly after six and pushed Mr. Coffee's button. After Anarchy left, the ceiling and I held an extended staring contest. The ceiling had won. I'd looked away first, resting my tired gaze on the alarm clock until its glowing red numbers turned fuzzy.

I must have drifted off, because lemony morning light woke me, leaving me in immediate need of caffeine.

Mr. Coffee gurgled happily. He didn't have to say the words —they were understood. *Coffee will make it all better.*

One could hope.

The dogs wagged their stubby tails and circled my legs.

I waded past wagging bodies to the back door. "Finn, no." The Airedale had taken to jumping on the door if I didn't open it fast enough to suit him. His nails were ruining my paint.

As soon as I had the door open, the dogs shot outside, speeding to the fence line. Every morning, they raced to the fence. Every morning, Max, our Weimaraner with plans for world domination, beat Finn. Every morning, Finn gave the race his all. Every morning, they both returned to the back door with huge grins on their doggy faces.

I scooped kibble into their bowls and put them on the floor. They'd expect breakfast the moment they came back inside. Then I refilled their water bowl.

There's enough for a cup.

I turned and offered Mr. Coffee the biggest smile I could muster, then I fetched a mug from the cabinet and the cream from the fridge.

Was there a sweeter sound than the splash of fresh-made coffee?

No, there was not.

I filled to just shy of the brim, added cream, and sighed. "Thank you."

My pleasure. Where did Anarchy go?

I glanced at the stairs leading to the second floor, where Grace and Beau still slept. With only ten days until school started again, Grace would linger in bed until ten, possibly eleven. Beau, who wasn't yet a teenager, might appear at any moment. "He caught a case. A body in the trunk of a car."

Look at the bright side. You didn't find the body.

"You're right." Mr. Coffee was right more often than not. "I'm grateful I didn't find the body. Especially because the car was parked at the club." If someone hadn't noticed the car in the middle of the night, I'd have gone to the club for my usual morning swim. It could easily have been me who peeked in that trunk.

Brnng, brnng.

"Jones' residence."

"It's me." My husband sounded cool, even distant. Off.

"Are you okay?" I asked. Anarchy never called when he was working.

"Fine. I'm calling from the clubhouse." He didn't add that someone was listening That I figured out for myself. "Do you know a man named Baxter Phelps?"

I imagined my husband standing at the receptionist's desk

with the phone pressed to his ear. I could almost see the tightness near his eyes and the way his lips narrowed.

"Yes." I might not have found the body, but I knew the corpse. And I could tell him what I knew. I tightened the belt on my seersucker bathrobe. "He's a lawyer. His wife's name is Helen."

"You're friends?"

"With Helen and Baxter? I wouldn't go that far. Helen and I have never met for lunch or played bridge, but we speak."

He must have heard something in my voice, because he asked, "You don't like her?"

"I like her just fine. She's…stiff. Actually, 'rigid' might be a better adjective. She draws within the lines. No imagination. No deviation from the norm. No…spark."

"And her husband?"

"They're well matched." I closed my eyes and took a breath. "It's his body?"

"Yes."

Max scratched at the back door, and I let the dogs in. They fell on their bowls like they hadn't eaten in weeks.

I rolled my eyes at their drama. "A mob hit?"

"Looks that way."

I shook my head in disbelief. "That makes no sense. Baxter is a respected tax attorney. Why would the mob kill him?" I settled onto a kitchen stool and wrapped the stretched-to-capacity phone cord around my right ring finger (Grace, in the name of privacy, had been known to stretch the cord across the kitchen—all the way to the backstairs, where she could close the door on whoever might listen to her top-secret teenage plans). "I can't imagine a circumstance where he'd encounter anyone connected to the mob." Much less do business with them.

"Single gunshot to the back of the head. Body in the trunk of his car."

"Was he killed at the club?"

"Doesn't look like it. The only blood is in the trunk. And there's not much. We think he was killed elsewhere and brought here."

"But?" I heard a note in his voice.

"But it's possible he was killed on the golf course. Uniforms are walking it as we speak."

"If they find anything?"

"We'll have to close the course."

That would go over like a lead balloon. In the heat of August, men played golf early in the day. Some men rose with the sun to get eighteen in before work. The uniform officers on the course were probably already causing delays. And righteous gnashing of teeth. And frustrated calls to the club president. And furious calls to the general manager. "Let's hope it doesn't come to that."

"A man is dead."

Again, I glanced at the clock. It was approaching six-thirty. "I don't think that will matter to the foursome with a seven o'clock tee time." I swirled the coffee in my cup. "It's odd."

"What's odd?"

"Why the club? Helen and Baxter aren't members."

"I have a theory."

"Oh?"

"There's an assistant prosecutor named Baxter Phillips."

"You think they killed the wrong Baxter?"

"From what you say, it's a possibility." Anarchy might be right, but that didn't explain why the killer had parked the car at the club.

I pulled the cord tight enough to whiten the tip of my finger. "I wonder…"

"What?"

"Baxter was a tax lawyer. Isn't the mob constantly dodging tax issues?" Even as I said the words, I dismissed them. Upright, uptight, dull Baxter Phelps and the mob? Not likely. Then again, people kept secrets. They did unexpected things. They surprised me.

"Good point. We'll definitely look into that. I've got to get back outside to the scene."

"Wait." I hated to keep Anarchy, but I needed a question answered.

"Yes?"

"Who found him?"

"The security guard. He chased off some kids who were pool hopping, then checked the parking lot to make sure they left."

"What attracted him to the car?" Club members who'd had one too many often left their cars in the lot overnight. A car in the lot wasn't enough to attract attention. Heck, the morning after the club's pool party, I'd counted thirty-two cars in the lot.

"The guard noticed the trunk was ajar. He worried someone's clubs had been stolen."

"Where was the car parked in the lot?"

"Near the first tee."

I went still. Near where I parked my car when I arrived early in the morning to swim. "I see."

"What's with the questions?"

A man was dead. Suggesting his killer left the body for me to find was narcissistic in the extreme. "Just wondering."

"I do have to get back out there."

"I understand. Love you."

"Love you, too." He hung up.

I was slow in replacing the receiver.

You okay? Mr. Coffee was always solicitous. Caring.

"Baxter Phelps is dead."

A friend?

"Not really. His wife Helen, she's a Cavanaugh, is six or seven years older than me. Her brother, Chipper, was a year ahead of me in high school. He took me to a school dance once."

My sister Marjorie, who was in Chipper's class, hadn't been pleased that her little sister was at *her* party.

Chipper?

"A chip off the old block. His given name is Rupert."

I see why he stuck with Chipper.

I nodded, remembering our date. Marjorie had lured Chipper away, and I'd found them kissing in the coat closet. Lifting my chin and surviving the rest of the evening had been excruciating. But I'd done it. Turned out that particular humiliation was great practice for being married to Henry. "Helen is best described as a stick in the mud. Likewise for Baxter."

Do you think she killed him?

"No idea." A surviving spouse was always a suspect. But putting Baxter's body in a trunk, then parking the car in the lot at the club required more imagination than Helen possessed. "Anarchy says there's a prosecutor named Baxter Phillips. It's possible they killed the wrong man."

But why park the car at the club?

Exactly! I could tell Mr. Coffee anything. He was always there for me. Steady. Comforting. Never judgmental. Still, I swallowed before I said, "I think the killer wanted me to find the body."

CHAPTER THREE

Beau held up red and blue binders. "Which one do you like?"

"Isn't red your favorite color?" I replied. We were shopping The Dime Store for school supplies. Binders. Folders. Pens. Paints. Pencils. Wide-ruled paper. Big Chief tablets. A lunchbox (I anticipated that decision would take a full twenty minutes—Scooby-Doo or Evel Knievel?). Markers. Sixty-four crayons. And a new backpack. I added a calculator to the basket I was putting together for Grace. She'd skipped our shopping trip. As a teenage girl, she cared about new clothes for school, not a new Trapper Data Center.

Behind me, the wooden floor creaked. Floors that creaked like they belonged in a haunted house were only a small part of The Dime Store's unique charm. The smell, reminiscent of my grandmother's attic—old paper, dust, and aged wood—was another selling point. Also, the store's big-hearted manager Bob Arfsten knew every customer by name. He'd greeted us when we entered, offering Beau a piece of penny candy as I perused shelves crammed with everything from kitchen gadgets to jigsaw puzzles to school supplies.

"Ellison?"

I knew that voice. Too well. Forcing a polite smile, I turned. "Jane, how nice to see you." Jane was a real estate agent determined to list my house. She didn't care that I had no plans to sell, she aggressively pursued the listing. Although, to be fair, since I'd married and welcomed Beau into our home, she'd backed off.

"Back-to-school shopping?" She smoothed her blue silk dress as her gaze took in Beau's overflowing basket.

Wasn't that obvious? Rather than answer her question, I said, "You look lovely. New dress?"

"I have a showing at eleven."

If she'd asked me, I'd have told her that the dress's neckline was too low for mornings or business or a woman who'd spent the past thirty years encouraging the sun to darken her chest the shade of saddle leather. She didn't ask. Instead, she took in my wrap skirt and scoop-necked tee and let her lips quirk. "I hear your husband is investigating the murder at the club."

"News travels fast."

"Baxter Phelps?"

"Yes."

She took a step closer, and the display case at my back kept me from retreating. Too bad, because Jane wore enough Youth Dew to make my eyes water. "Helen and Baxter were having trouble."

"Were they?" I tried to breathe through my mouth.

"Just last month, Helen asked how much their house was worth. I told her we'd need a pricing opinion."

"A what?"

"I'd ask a few other agents to walk through and give their opinions. She backed off immediately and asked me not to mention her interest to anyone."

Yet, here we were, discussing it in the school-supply aisle at The Dime Store.

"I've been doing this a long time. When a wife asks how much the house is worth, she's thinking of leaving."

"Why are you telling me?"

She simpered. "Your husband might be interested."

True. But that didn't answer my question. Why was Jane throwing Helen to the wolves? Especially when the newly widowed Helen might downsize. I put the basket full of Grace's school supplies on the floor and crossed my arms as I lifted my brows.

We stared at each other, long enough for me to notice a clump in Jane's mascara.

"Fine," she huffed as the floor creaked beneath her shifting weight. "Helen was never going to list with me. Her best friend is an agent. Obviously, Helen didn't want to admit her marital troubles to perfect Lindsey. But, when push came to shove, Helen would have listed with her. Not me. I figure, this way, you owe me a favor."

I didn't owe her a thing. My tight smile said as much. "I'll pass your theory on to Anarchy."

Beau dropped the red binder and a Scooby-Doo lunchbox into his basket. "That's it."

"Rubber cement?" When Grace was in grade school, I forgot rubber cement for three years running. The teachers whispered about me—the artist who forgot art supplies. I even got a call. One that still made my stomach tighten with dread. The principal (the principal!) had reminded me that my hobby (I had a successful career as an artist) wasn't as important as my real job (mothering). What's more, as an artist, I should understand the importance of art supplies.

As an artist, I'd never used rubber cement. For anything. But the art teacher did. Affixing third-grade masterpieces to mat boards.

Beau shook his blond head. "I'll go get some."

He scampered off.

"You're a saint to take in that boy."

"Not at all. He's a delight."

"Who's not yours."

Beau was absolutely ours. But arguing with Jane was a worthless endeavor, almost as hopeless as arguing with Mother. I offered up another tight smile. Paired it with a narrow-eyed stare. Her opinion, such as it was, was not welcome.

Jane tugged at the collar of her too revealing dress. "I'll let you get back to your shopping. Toodles." She waggled her fingers at me and turned toward the register where she purchased a package of Polaroid film.

I waited until she was gone before hauling Beau's overflowing basket along with Grace's supplies to the smiling white-haired woman who ran the register.

"Good morning, Mrs. Jones."

"Good morning." I should know her name—Mary? Marian? Marla?

She entered the lunchbox's price into the register. "Such a bittersweet time of year. The kids are excited for school to start. Parents, too."

Beau joined us at the counter and added a brown jar to his loot. "I got the last jar."

I ruffled his hair. The principal would not call. That was a good thing.

"New supplies." The checker (what was her name?) entered the rubber cement's price. "New clothes. New things to learn. But I always look at it as the death of summer." Something about the way she said "death" sent a shiver down my spine.

"It's just a change of seasons."

"But autumn is the season when things die."

Another shiver gripped my spine. "It's also the season for football and apple cider and Halloween." Soon, Ben Sherman boxed costumes would replace school supplies on The Dime Store's wooden shelves.

"You're right. But there are also dead leaves and dead flowers and—"

Dead bodies. The little voice in my head was *not* helpful.

CHAPTER FOUR

A ggie, our housekeeper, was a gem.

Before I took Beau shopping, I wrote her a note telling her what I needed, and she'd baked a gorgeous Bundt cake. Chocolate drizzled with luscious ganache.

I carefully balanced the cake against my hip and jabbed Helen Phelps' doorbell with my free hand. Then, I waited. The August sun beat on my exposed neck, and I felt a trickle of sweat between my shoulder blades.

After an eternity (a full minute), the door swung open.

"Ellison." Helen looked pale beneath her tan, and the puffiness around her eyes spoke of tears.

"I'm so sorry for your loss." I held out Aggie's cake.

She scowled at the cake plate as if I were offering her a platter of wriggling maggots.

"It's chocolate."

Her expression didn't change.

"If I've caught you at a bad time…"

"No. No." Helen shook her head slowly, as if she'd come to an unpleasant decision. "You'd better come in." She didn't sound best pleased, but she did open the door wider and stepped aside so I could enter. Then, she took Aggie's cake from my hands.

The Phelps's foyer was painted a soft beige. A worn Heriz rug in shades of beige and coral covered the hardwood floors.

"This way." Helen led me to her living room. It was tastefully decorated in soft blues, creams, and beige. "Have a seat. May I offer you an iced tea?"

"That would be lovely." I chose a blue velvet wingback chair and sat. "Thank you."

She gave a brief nod and disappeared.

I glanced around the room. Watercolors in gilt frames graced the walls, another Heriz (slightly less worn than the one in the foyer) spread across the floor, and photographs in simple frames covered the closed lid of a baby grand piano.

I rose from my chair and perused the photos. Most of them were of Helen and Baxter's daughter, Jessica. Like her parents, Jessica had a serious face. Her smiles seemed tentative.

"We just got back from taking her to school. She's a senior at Princeton."

"Smart girl. You must be very proud."

"Baxter's alma mater." Helen put a tray holding two glasses, a pitcher, a sugar bowl, and a bowl of lemon slices on the coffee table. "He burst his buttons when she was admitted. Lemon or sugar?"

"Lemon." I returned to my chair and accepted the proffered glass of tea. "Thank you."

"I should be thanking you. For the cake, for taking time to visit. It was kind of you to come." Helen didn't sound thankful. She sounded exhausted.

"I don't mean to intrude." Where were Helen's close friends? Why was she alone?

"I'm glad for the company. I...I can't believe this is real." She glanced down at her lap. "How did you feel when Henry died?"

I'd run over my husband's body. The sickening thwomp of tires rolling over flesh had been more traumatic than his actual death. At least for me. "I was so worried about Grace that I didn't take time to analyze my feelings. She adored her father."

The doorbell chimed, and Helen slumped on her couch. For a brief second, she covered her face with her hands and her shoulders shook. A second guest was the straw that might break the camel's back.

"Would you like me to answer that?"

"Would you? Please?" She sounded ridiculously hopeful.

"Of course." Remembering the way the sun beat on my neck when I stood on the stoop, I hurried to the front door. When I opened it, I found Jinx George and Sandy Wilcox on the other side. Jinx, who was a dear friend, held a casserole dish. Sandy, who was an acquaintance, carried a grocery bag.

Jinx's brows lifted as if my presence came as a surprise. "Ellison."

I leaned forward and kissed the air next to her cheek. "Come in out of the heat."

The two women stepped into the foyer.

"Sandy, it's lovely to see you. Helen is in the living room."

Sandy held up her bag. "This needs to be refrigerated. I brought her a few quarts of gazpacho. I'll say 'hello' than stow this in the fridge."

Jinx and I watched her swan into the living room. And she did swan. Sandy was tall and willowy and graceful. She knelt next to Helen and wrapped her long arms around her friend's shoulders. Maybe she didn't notice the way Helen stiffened, but I saw it from across the room.

"What are you doing here?" Jinx's voice was low, barely a whisper.

"Aggie made a Bundt." That didn't answer her question. Not at all. Helen and I were friendly, not friends. But Anarchy was investigating her husband's murder, and I felt obligated to put in an appearance.

"What kind?" Aggie's Bundt cakes had reached legendary status, and Jinx's eyes lit with enthusiasm she usually reserved for hot gossip.

"Chocolate."

Her eyes glinted with interest. "Really? Has Helen cut it yet?"

"No."

"I'll work on that." Jinx strode into the living room. "Helen, how are you? I brought a chicken and wild rice casserole. Just pop it in the oven for thirty minutes to warm it up."

Helen blinked, then roused herself. "Thank you. You and Sandy are so kind."

"Of course," Jinx replied. "We're so sorry for your loss. You look pale. Have you eaten?"

Helen hesitated, as if the question required thought. "No."

"Ellison mentioned she brought cake. I'll cut you a slice." She scanned the coffee table. "And I'll bring more glasses."

Jinx and Sandy disappeared, leaving me with Helen.

She wrung her hands. "More will come."

"Yes."

"It's kind of them, but I need time to...I don't know... breathe. Process. Understand what's happened. Who would kill Baxter?" She stared at me as if she expected an answer.

"You'd know better than me."

Her gaze dropped to her hands. "Black coffee. Wheat toast. Soft-boiled egg. Every morning. A single scotch and soda every night. Why kill a man like that?"

"Something at work?"

She scoffed. "No. It must be a mistake. It just can't be."

Denial. I'd been there. Often. "Helen—"

She held up her left hand, stopping me. "I know he's dead. I know there's no mistake about that. What I'm saying is that someone killed the wrong man." She sounded more bemused than sad.

The other Baxter. Baxter Phillips. Was Anarchy right? Then, I thought of Jane's revelation. "When Henry died, we were more like roommates than husband and wife."

She nodded as if she understood exactly what I wasn't saying. "Black coffee. Wheat toast. Soft-boiled egg. We had a routine. We were like broken-in slippers."

It all sounded dreadfully boring to me. But my life was a roller-coaster of dead bodies and a love that hadn't had time to mellow. My days were shot through with adrenalin and passion.

"Not terribly exciting, but it worked for us."

"Cake!" Jinx carried two dessert plates; each held a generous slice of Bundt cake. She gave the larger slice to Helen. "Have you ever tasted Aggie's cake? Ellison's housekeeper puts Betty Crocker and Duncan Hines to shame."

Slowly, as if the fork weighed a hundred pounds, Helen lifted a bite of cake to her lips.

"Ellison?" Sandy stood at the entrance to the living room. "Do you want cake?"

"No, thank you."

"This is marvelous." Helen lifted a second bite.

"I'm glad you like it."

Sandy lingered in the entrance. "Would you please help me carry in the glasses?"

I stood. "Of course."

Helen's kitchen featured linoleum floors, baby blue cabinets, and cream countertops. Sandy stood next to an open cabinet that held glasses. "Can you believe this kitchen? It hasn't been touched since 1956. Baxter wouldn't let her update."

"Why not?"

Sandy held up her hand and rubbed her thumb against her first two fingers. "He was a tightwad. Had the first dollar he ever made. He gave Helen a pittance for an allowance. If not for the money from her grandparents' trust, she and Jessica would have wardrobes from K-Mart. It was one of the major problems in their marriage."

"Oh?"

"If you ask me, the bigger problem was that he was dull as dishwater. If you'll grab the glasses, please?" Sandy picked up a plate topped with a slice of Aggie's cake and a stack of cocktail napkins.

I grabbed two iced tea glasses and followed her back to the living room where she joined Helen on the couch.

Sandy ate a bite of cake, moaned, then asked, "Helen, what can we do to help you?"

"I honestly don't know." Death when one wasn't expecting it was overwhelming. There was the grief, yes, but there was also an obituary to write, a funeral to plan, and, in our crowd, a reception at the country club. Failing a reception, there would be cookies and punch in the church basement. "Where do I start?"

"Plan the funeral," I told her. "Then write the obit."

Tears welled in her eyes. The first tears I'd seen from her. "It just seems like too much."

Sandy patted her arm. "I'll help. I planned Daddy's funeral a few months ago."

"You'd do that?" A single tear ran unchecked down Helen's pale cheek.

"Of course. What are friends for?" Sandy picked up her plate and ate another bite of cake. "Ellison, does your housekeeper share her recipes?"

"No."

She looked up from her plate. "You're sure? Not even with friends?"

Sandy and I weren't exactly friends—more like friendly acquaintances. "Not even then."

She wrinkled her nose and turned her attention to Helen. "What happened? To Baxter, I mean."

"They found his body in the trunk of a car."

Jinx nodded as if Helen had confirmed information already received.

"Weren't you worried when he didn't come home?" asked Sandy.

Helen flushed a dull red. "Baxter snored like a freight train. We haven't shared a bedroom in years."

"Where was he last night?" I asked.

"He told me he was having dinner with Lloyd Crowder. Said he'd be late. I watched a program on television, then went to bed. Probably around ten."

Sandy and Jinx exchanged a telling glance, and I could almost hear their silent conversation.

Sandy's lips narrowed with disapproval. *There's another woman!*

Possibly. Jinx never jumped to conclusions. Instead, she gathered facts and waited for confirmation.

Who stays out late discussing tax law? Especially with Lloyd Crowder. Sandy was right about that. Lloyd was every bit as boring as Baxter.

That didn't mean they were right about Baxter having a mistress. I took a small sip of Helen's too-strong tea. "Where did Baxter and Lloyd meet?"

"Baxter said they were meeting at Lloyd's club."

My club. The club where his body was found. Maybe Baxter had been meeting with Lloyd. Lloyd's wife Elizabeth and I were friends. With a phone call, I could easily find out if he spent last evening with Baxter.

Anarchy, who was focused on the mob angle of Baxter's death, would appreciate my asking questions of club members.

And pigs flew.

CHAPTER FIVE

I sat at my desk in the family room and flipped through my
well-worn address book, stopping when I found Elizabeth
Crowder's number.

"Mom?" Grace's voice carried from the kitchen.

"In the family room," I called.

A moment later, my daughter stood in the room's cased
entrance. Grace had my late husband's determined eyes and
Mother's even-more determined chin. She wanted something.

I braced myself.

She offered me a hopeful grin. "Can we go shopping?"

"Now? I thought we were going tomorrow. I have the whole
day reserved."

Back-to-school shopping with Grace was a marathon, not a
sprint. We'd go to the Plaza and hit Harzfeld's and Woolf Brothers
and Swanson's. We might visit the same store twice, even three
times. We'd stop for a light lunch. We might make multiple trips
to the car to stash shopping bags. I'd asked Beau if he wanted to
come, and he'd turned me down with alacrity. Waiting while
Grace tried on outfit after outfit was not his idea of fun.

Instead, we'd gone through his drawers and closet and determined that he needed new khakis, shirts, jeans, socks and underwear. He trusted me to buy it all. He did want to go shoe shopping, but that could wait for another day.

"You don't want to get a head start?" she wheedled. "I thought we might run out to Stix." She meant Stix, Baer & Fuller. The store, which anchored the Ward Parkway mall, was a favorite. Mother adored their tearoom where svelte models showcased elegant ensembles during lunch. I liked the store's children's department. If we went, I could make a dent in Beau's list.

Very tempting. "I have to make a call first."

"Mom." She turned the word into a lament.

"What?"

"You'll be on the phone for hours."

"I won't."

She rolled her eyes so far; she probably saw the back of her head.

"We can go tomorrow," I offered.

A woe-is-me expression settled on Grace's pretty face. "We're going to the Plaza tomorrow."

"The day after?" I suggested.

"Pool with Debbie and Peggy."

"So, what you're saying is the next few hours are the only time we can go to Stix." I barely hid a smile.

"Yes!" So. Much. Teenage. Angst.

The smile almost broke through. Luckily, I clenched my jaw just in time. "If we don't make it this afternoon, we'll find a time. Is there something specific you want?"

"Jeans. I *need* them." She made the need sound desperate, as if covering her legs in denim when the thermometer pushed past ninety degrees was of immediate importance.

I stared at her until she flushed and lowered her gaze.

"Fine," she huffed. "Make your call. But remember, it isn't easy to find jeans that fit."

My favorite saleswoman at Swanson's assured me it was only a matter of time until designers started jeans lines. If Grace thought buying jeans was hard now...

"You will have jeans in time to start school." Not that she'd even wear them. The first few weeks of September were too hot for denim. "I promise."

"What's for dinner?" she asked. My friends, who weren't fortunate to have someone like Aggie, swore that was the worst question ever asked.

The question didn't bother me. "Aggie's roasting a chicken."

"And?"

"You'd have to ask her."

"Fine." Grace turned on her heel and left me.

I picked up the receiver and dialed Elizabeth's number.

"Crowder residence."

"Elizabeth? It's Ellison Jones on the line."

"Ellison! How lovely to hear your voice! How are you?"

"Fine, thank you. How are you?" The rote exchange of polite inquiries was comforting.

"Just devastated to hear about Baxter Phelps. He met Lloyd for a drink last night, and now he's dead. I heard he was strangled and dumped in the lot at the country club."

I didn't correct the details. "It's such a tragedy. Did Lloyd meet Baxter at the club?"

"No. That's the crazy thing. They met at the bar at Nabil's. I joined them around six-thirty, then Lloyd and I had dinner there."

"Baxter didn't join you?"

"No."

Baxter had lied to Helen. Or Helen had lied to me. Either way, Baxter had not spent the evening with Lloyd.

"Say, will I see you tomorrow night?"

"The Brandts' party? Yes."

"Marvelous. Can we chat then? You caught me in the middle of making dinner."

"So sorry."

"Not at all. It's always a pleasure to talk to you. We'll catch up tomorrow. Bye for now."

"Goodbye." I hung up the receiver and tilted my head, staring at the ceiling. Where had Baxter gone when he left Lloyd and Elizabeth? To meet a mistress as Jinx and Sandy suspected? Or somewhere more sinister?

CHAPTER SIX

"What do you think?" Grace stepped out of the dressing room wearing a short twill skirt and a flowered blouse. It was easily the fiftieth outfit she'd tried on.

"I like it." The skirt was long enough that she wouldn't get sent home from school. "You can wear that skirt with lots of tops."

"So, it's a yes?"

"It's a yes."

She returned to the dressing room.

"Another coffee, Mrs. Jones?"

I gave Leota, our saleswoman at Harzfeld's, a grateful smile. "Please."

A moment later, she put a fresh cup on the glass-top side table next to my chair. The small seating area outside the dressing rooms was elegant. Chairs covered in rich brocade, delicate tables that held copies of *Vogue* and the latest issues of *The Independent*. Deep thick carpet. Hushed tones and the scent of fine fabric. I sighed with contentment as I took a sip from the porcelain cup.

"Your daughter is a delight."

"Thank you for saying so."

"It's true. I've seen knock-down drag-outs between mothers and daughters. Just yesterday we had a shouting match." Leota, who was almost birdlike, puffed up like a robin in springtime. "It was shocking."

I offered a weak smile. "The skirt was too short?"

"Too tight. The girl gained some weight over the summer."

I winced. Mothers and daughters and appearances were always a minefield. I could say the most innocuous thing to Grace, and she'd hear criticism that wasn't there. I probably did the same thing with Mother...no, Mother meant every critical word that passed her lips. She believed I was a reflection of her and her mothering skills. And even now, as I closed in on forty, she wasn't shy about telling me how to dress, act, or comport myself.

Grace emerged from the dressing room carrying a large pile of clothes.

"May I take those?" Leota asked.

"Thank you." Grace handed over her haul.

I handed over my charge plate and stood. "Next stop Woolf's?" We'd already hit Swanson's.

Grace nodded, and we wandered back onto the sales floor. Mannequins were posed next to the clothes they wore, soft music played in the background, and a handful of well-dressed shoppers perused the merchandise.

Grace paused and frowned.

"What's wrong?" I asked.

"That man. I saw him at Swanson's."

I followed her gaze.

A man with dark hair and bronzed skin stood next to a round of women's blouses. He wore black pants, a black shirt, and dark sunglasses. When he noticed me staring, he gave a curt nod and turned away.

"Maybe he's shopping for his wife."

Grace rolled her eyes.

I couldn't blame her. The man did not look like a typical Harzfeld's shopper.

Leota finished ringing up Grace's new clothes, then she folded each item neatly before wrapping it in the store's signature tissue. The process was painstakingly slow.

Grace, who had the patience of a typical teenager, whispered, "May I go look at shoes?"

"Go."

A few minutes later, with two large green-and-white striped bags in each hand, I found Grace trying on clogs with chunky wooden heels. "Don't you have a pair just like that?"

"Not in this color."

With my Harzfeld's card already begging for mercy, I said, "Let's look at Woolf Brothers before we make any decisions." Then I smiled at the salesman kneeling at Grace's feet. "Would you please put the clogs on hold for us? Also—" I pointed at a pair of gorgeous stacked-heel boots in a rich burgundy leather "—those in a size seven." I couldn't resist boots. Grace couldn't resist clogs. But, until I checked our closets for something similar, I wasn't buying. "My name is Ellison Jones; I'll call you when we get home."

"Of course, Mrs. Jones." He handed me his card, which I slipped into my handbag.

Then, Grace and I stepped onto the sidewalk where the heat pressed against us—sticky, cloying, horrible. Locusts droned louder than lawnmowers, and the sun seemed determined to melt me into a pile of goo.

"Let's put these in the car and drive to Woolf's."

Grace nodded, and we hurried around the corner to the parking lot.

Despite being covered, the three-story lot was hot as blazes, the concrete trapping the heat like an oven. So why did a shiver travel my spine? I looked over my shoulder and saw nothing but parked cars. "Hurry up, Grace."

"Why? What's wrong?" Thankfully, she walked faster.

"Nothing. A feeling."

We reached the car, crammed the bags into the trunk, climbed in and locked the doors. With shaking fingers, I slid the key in the ignition and started the car.

I didn't draw an easy breath until we reached the street. "I didn't mean to scare you. I'm probably being silly…"

"I trust your hunches, Mom. Do you want to go home?"

This was our day, and I wouldn't let a moment's panic in the parking lot ruin it. "No, but let's look for a spot on the street."

We circled Woolf's block twice before a parking spot opened up. As I backed in, I asked, "What else you need?"

"Besides jeans?"

"Besides jeans."

"I'm not sure. Let's see what they have." Dangerous words.

I'd made Grace go through her closet before the shopping trip. She'd purged too-short shorts, too-tight dresses, pilled sweaters, and too-small pants. Easily three-quarters of the clothes she'd worn to school last year were bagged, waiting to be taken to the Junior League thrift shop.

"Look, Mom. It's him. The man in black."

The man we'd seen at Harzfeld's carried a green-and-white-striped shopping bag. As we watched, he ducked into Woolf's.

"At least we know he's not following us."

I nodded. Slowly. Had he heard me mention Woolf's was our next stop? Was I being paranoid because Anarchy was investigating the mob? Probably. "Why don't we grab a bite to eat before we hit Woolf's?"

"You're worried about that man." There were no flies on Grace.

How much should I tell her? "Anarchy's investigating a potential mob hit, and—"

"Everyone knows that, Mom. It's why I noticed him."

Alrighty then. "Nabil's?" We were nearby, and I adored their chicken with lemon and capers.

We walked the short block to the restaurant. This was our day. Just the two of us. And I intended to enjoy it. I pushed aside the feeling of dread that had hit me in the parking lot, along with Baxter's murder, the man in black, and the impending Harzfeld's bill.

CHAPTER SEVEN

Perry welcomed Anarchy and me to his home with a quick kiss on my cheek. "Ellison, you look lovely. So glad you could join us."

"Thank you for including us."

"Are you kidding? It wouldn't be a party without you." He held out his hand to Anarchy, and the two men shook. "I hear you're having an exciting week."

Anarchy offered up a mild give-nothing-away smile. "Nothing out of the ordinary."

"A mob hit at the country club is definitely out of the ordinary."

Next to me Anarchy stiffened slightly—a movement so tiny that Perry probably didn't notice. I noticed. Really, Anarchy shouldn't be surprised that Perry knew about the investigation. The grapevine was efficient—and voracious—and Baxter Phelps' murder was big news. The surprise would be if Perry didn't know about the murder.

"Call me if you want to know more about Baxter Phelps." Perry's satisfied tone said he had gossip to spill. Men said women were gossips, but I found male of the species to be even more likely to tittle-tattle. Of course, they didn't call it gossip. But it was.

"First thing Monday morning," Anarchy replied.

The two men stared at each other, holding a silent conversation.

Too bad I can't tell you now. Perry looked almost gleeful. Whatever he knew was juicy.

I agree.

Oh, dear Lord. I got it. They didn't want to discuss murder at a party. Frankly, I didn't either. But the hosts, the homicide detective, and I were probably the only ones who didn't.

"Chester is tending bar in the living room." It was a gentle nudge, allowing Perry to greet whoever was making their way up his front walk.

Chester served bar at most of the parties I attended. It was no surprise when he greeted me with a smile and asked, "Your usual, Mrs. Jones?"

"Please." I drank gin and tonics with two limes in the summertime.

"For you, detective?"

"Seltzer."

I lifted a brow.

"Technically, I'm working." He patted the spot on his belt where his navy sports coat covered a pager.

Anarchy had been working non-stop since the security guard at the club found Baxter's body. He'd climbed into bed in the wee hours and left before I got up. I'd left a message to remind him of the party and was half-surprised when he made it home to get ready.

Unfortunately, we hadn't had time to chat. No update on the case. No mention of the man in black. Instead, already dressed for the party, I'd given Beau a ride to Bobby Woodson's house. Bobby's dad, Rob, was taking the boys to the Woodson's country house for the weekend. They'd fish and ride horses and swing in hammocks. They'd shoot bb guns and swim in the pond and count the stars. Beau would have a marvelous time. I missed him already.

When I'd returned home from the drop-off, it was time to leave for the party, and the few short blocks to the Brandts' home hadn't allowed us enough time to catch up.

"Are you carrying a gun?" I whispered.

Chester's brows shot upwards, and Anarchy claimed my elbow and steered me away from the bar. I noticed he hadn't answered me.

We paused near a seating area—cream velvet-covered club chairs and a butler's tray coffee table holding a sterling silver julep cup filled with cigarettes, crystal ashtrays, and a plethora of needlepoint coasters.

"Ellison!" Elizabeth Crowder called to me from across the living room. Unlike her staid husband, Elizabeth was vivacious. Fun. A personality. Tonight, she wore an orange and pink silk muumuu with a cascade of turquoise around her neck. The turquoise couldn't be real. That many stones would have her hunched over like a crone. Real or paste, she looked stylish.

"Give me a minute," Leaving Anarchy, I met her in the center of the room, and we exchanged air kisses.

"Your dress is fabulous," she exclaimed.

With Labor Day looming, I'd taken the opportunity to wear the white dress I'd bought at Chaven when Grace and I visited Paris last summer. It was light and airy and perfect for a humid night in August. "Paris," I told her.

"I wish Lloyd would take me to Paris."

"You have more style in your little finger than half the women in France."

"It's kind of you to say, but I'd still like to go."

"You both look wonderful." Libba had joined us. My best friend wore—no surprise—a halter dress with a plunging neck-line and clutched a martini glass like it might try to escape if she loosened her hold on the stem. "Ellison, what can you tell us about Baxter's murder?"

"Nothing."

She wrinkled her nose at me. "Don't be stingy."

"I'm not. I don't know a thing. I've hardly seen Anarchy since the body was found."

We all turned our heads and found Anarchy. He was chatting with Lloyd. My husband was tall and fit and gorgeous. Lloyd was not.

"Lloyd has been so bothered about Baxter's death. I'm glad he got a chance to chat with your husband." There were hearts in Elizabeth's eyes as she stared at Lloyd. I saw a middle-aged man with a thickening waist, thinning hair, and sun-reddened cheeks. She saw the love of her life. She was a lucky woman. Too many of our friends merely tolerated their husbands.

"Look at those cheeks." Elizabeth shook her head. "Lloyd golfed this afternoon—thank heavens they re-opened the course so quickly. Of course, he forgot his hat. His dermatologist is going to scold him."

"Brad Quinn?"

"Yes."

Brad had lectured me about the dangers of too much sun. I did my very best not to burn, but there was something so relaxing about sunning on a chaise at the pool. Especially now, at the end of the season, when kids were tired of swimming and their ranks were thinned.

"He scolds everyone," Libba replied. "He warned me I'd have skin like a crocodile by the time I'm sixty. Pfft."

"You don't care?" I asked.

"I'll be a tanned, fabulous crocodile."

"Of course you will."

Libba narrowed her eyes as if she doubted sincerity.

I turned back to Elizabeth. "Did you find out what Baxter and Lloyd discussed at Nabil's?"

Her smile faltered, and she adjusted one of the necklaces circling her throat. "Lloyd says it's privileged." Meaning he couldn't tell her what they talked about.

"Privileged? Baxter hired Lloyd?"

Elizabeth tugged at one of the turquoise necklaces. "I really couldn't say."

Couldn't or wouldn't? Why did she look so nervous?

"Did Baxter and Lloyd meet often?" I asked.

"No." She scanned the room. "Would you please excuse me? I must speak with Prudence."

"Of course." As Elizabeth hurried away, I wondered what she was hiding. No one voluntarily chatted with Prudence Davies. The woman was bitter as wormwood, mean as an asp, and had teeth that would make Mr. Ed jealous.

"I have news." Libba, who wasn't remotely curious as to why Elizabeth was avoiding our conversation, took a large sip from her martini glass.

"Oh?" I'd known Libba since we could toddle. "News," might be a planned shopping trip to New York, a Mexican vacation with my neighbor and her beau, Charlie Ardmore, or a new manicurist.

"Charlie wants to get married."

"What?" I was loud enough to draw attention. I lowered my voice and asked, "You're serious?" *This* was news. Big news. Libba had spent the past twenty years avoiding marriage. I stared at her, taking in her perfect tan, expertly applied make-up, and the slightly panicked look in her eyes. "What are you going to do?"

"I don't know. I adore Charlie. I do. But he's freshly divorced, and his kids don't exactly like me, and I never considered marriage." She swirled the last sip of her drink. "It's not for me."

"Tell me you're considering Charlie's proposal. Please."

She drained the last drop of her martini, then stared into her empty glass. "Yes. No. Maybe."

"What did you say when he asked?"

"I told him I love him, but I need time to think."

"And?"

"He told me to take my time."

I wasn't surprised. Charlie adored Libba. I had a feeling he'd wait for her till the end of time.

Libba took a step toward Chester and another martini. "May I come over tomorrow morning? I really need to talk this out."

There went my lazy Saturday. "Of cou—"

"Ellison. Twice in one day!" Sandy Wilcox had joined us. "Libba—" she kissed the air next to Libba's cheek "—you look gorgeous."

"Thank you. That's a pretty dress you have on." Libba didn't like pretty dresses. She liked provocative dresses, statement dresses, jaw-dropping dresses.

Sandy smoothed chiffon over her slender hips. The fabric of her turquoise dress was dotted with royal blue flowers. A modest square neckline and fluttery sleeves made it the type of garment Libba wouldn't wear on a bet. "I picked this up at Gump's when Grant took me on his business trip last month."

"Very pretty." I ignored Libba's small cough. "Did you enjoy San Francisco?"

"Union Square is fabulous. Grant insisted on taking a tour of Alcatraz. I couldn't imagine why he wanted to visit a prison, but we took the ferry and saw Al Capone's cell."

"How was it?" asked Libba.

"Depressing. If I never visit another prison, it'll be too soon. I much preferred Ghiradelli's."

"Ghee, like the clarified butter, not jee." Libba was in a mood. Normally she wouldn't correct someone's pronunciation. Charlie's proposal had thrown her for a loop.

Sandy waved away Libba's snarky reply. "Tomato, tomahto."

Libba's lips thinned, and I could sense the sharp retort poised on the tip of her barbed tongue. I grabbed her arm. "Would you look at that! Chester's free. Sandy, please excuse us." With my fingers holding tight, I pulled Libba toward the bar. Not that it took much effort. Libba. Bar.

"I can't stand that woman."

"Why ever not?"

"She just rubs me the wrong way. And that dress? Gump's wouldn't sell that dress on a bet. More like Filene's Basement, and that might be generous."

Chester refreshed our drinks.

When we thanked him and turned away from the bar, Grant Wilcox stood behind us.

Had he heard Libba disparaging his wife? His smile didn't reach his pale blue eyes, so I was guessing *yes*.

"Grant, how nice to see you." In uncomfortable situations, I turned to rote politeness.

He leaned forward and brushed a kiss across my cheek. "Ellison, what a pretty dress." He'd definitely heard us.

Rather than thank him, I gritted my teeth to trap a nervous, highly inappropriate laugh.

His blue eyes narrowed. "Libba, nice to see you too."

"You think Ellison's dress is pretty?"

Grant blinked as if Libba's unexpected question had caught him unawares. "You don't?"

Arguably, my dress was pretty.

"Ellison expresses herself through her clothes. So, yes, the dress might be pretty—" she cast me a side-eye "—and from last season, but ultimately, it's stylish."

Grant's cheeks flushed.

"She bought it at Chaven in Paris. The original design called for harvest-gold silk, but Ellison had it custom-made in white." Libba was lying through her perfect teeth.

I shot my best friend a death glare. I understood she was in a mood but taking it out on Grant wasn't fair. "Sandy was just telling us about your visit to Alcatraz." My words tripped over each other in my eagerness to change the subject.

"Fascinating place. Grim. But I bet you know all about prisons."

I gaped at him. Why would he think that? "Oh?"

"Being married to a cop."

"Anarchy puts murderers in jail. We don't visit them afterwards."

He chuckled, then rubbed a palm across his chin. "I heard he's investigating Baxter Phelps' death."

"Yes."

He leaned close to me, his *Pour Homme* cologne assaulting my nose. "Your husband should look into Baxter's habit."

"What habit?"

He leaned closer still. "Baxter gambled."

Bland Baxter Phelps. Dull Baxter Phelps. Boring Baxter Phelps had a secret dark side? "He did?"

"Yep." He popped the "p."

"On what?" Libba looked at Grant as if he was trying to sell her ocean-front property in Lawrence, Kansas.

He frowned at her interruption. "Sports. This time of year, it's baseball. Football in the fall. Basketball in the winter. Horses in the spring."

Plenty of men gambled. Daddy gambled when he played golf. And one of his oldest friends from college had box seats at Churchill Downs. I was sure Daddy placed bets when he and Mother went to the Derby.

"His gambling was a problem?" I exchanged a this-can't-be-true glance with Libba.

Had the mob killed him because he owed them money? No. That didn't make sense. They couldn't recoup money from a dead man. Unless someone had made an example of him.

"For years. The house is in Helen's name so he can't borrow against it."

"Why would a tax attorney gamble?" Libba asked.

The same reason a CEO drank himself blind drunk or a well-to-do housewife popped diet pills. Addiction didn't care about job titles or affluence. "You're sure about this?"

Grant nodded. "Positive. I made the mistake of loaning him money several years ago."

"How did he keep it quiet?" Surely, I would have heard about a gambling addiction.

"It's an open secret. At least among the men in our set." His gaze swept the room, and a satisfied smirk settled onto his face when his gaze landed on Anarchy.

Grant had no business looking so smug. His father had made a fortune manufacturing padded toilet seats—more than enough to send his son to private schools. Grant had made friends (boys overlooked toilet seat money if the beneficiary was a good athlete). Men did too, especially when that the toilet-seat-maker picked up rounds at the nineteenth hole.

Women were less forgiving. Grant wasn't a member of the old guard. He wasn't in our set. At best, he was adjacent. I refrained from saying that aloud. One, it was snooty. Two, it sounded too much like Mother. Three, I'd married someone from outside our set and I was gloriously happy. "I'll be sure and mention the gambling to Anarchy."

"Something a policeman should know." The way Grant said *policeman*—like he was somehow better than Anarchy—made me want to bring him down several pegs. Mother would. She'd eviscerate anyone who spoke disparagingly of Daddy. I wasn't my mother, and Grant wasn't worth the effort.

"If you'll excuse me, I should find Sandy." Grant turned on his heel and left us, but not before I noticed the smarmy, self-congratulatory smile on his tanned face.

"That was odd." Libba narrowed her eyes at his retreating back.

"What?"

"He never ordered a drink." She was right. After waiting in line behind us, Grant had left empty-handed.

"He wanted to tell us about the gambling."

"Seltzer with lime."

We turned back toward the bar where our friend Jinx was getting a drink. When Chester handed her a highball, she lifted the glass in a mock toast. "Cheers, girls."

We clinked glasses and sipped our drinks.

"Any news on the murder?" Jinx asked. That seemed to be the question of the night.

I shook my head. "Anarchy and I have hardly had a moment."

She pursed her lips, disappointed I couldn't share a juicy tidbit. Not that I would. I kept any details Anarchy shared with me to myself.

"Do you know anything about Baxter Phelps' gambling?"

Jinx's eyes went shifty. "I might have heard about it."

"And?"

"And nothing. I never asked. Gambling is an addiction." Jinx had her own addiction. It made sense that she didn't want to poke at someone else's. "Are you going to Marilyn Tremblay's luncheon on Monday?"

"I am. Have you learned anything more about Donna Miller?" The engraved invitation had arrived weeks ago. A luncheon at a home that wasn't Marilyn's, co-hosted by a woman I'd never heard of. I assumed from the address on the invitation that Donna Miller and her husband were the new owners of the Winfield's house—an enormous Tudor on a quiet street in old Mission Hills. I didn't have reason to pass the house often, but when I did, the driveway was filled with pickup trucks and panel vans, and workmen scurried around the house like carpenter ants. "Have you met her?"

"No one has. Well, no one but Marilyn. Apparently, the son is dating Emma Tremblay."

"It must be serious if his parents bought a house here."

Jinx clinked the ice in her glass. "There should be a ring any day now. Marilyn wants Donna to meet her friends before they invite anyone to the engagement party."

"Do the Millers have other children?" The Winfield house had seven bedrooms.

"Not that I know of. I'm just glad someone is putting some money into the place. It needed it." In the latter years of her life, Sally Winfield had let her mansion go to seed.

Libba lit a cigarette and blew a plume of smoke at the ceiling. "I can't wait to see what they've done with the house."

Jinx nodded. "It will give us something to talk about besides Baxter Phelps' murder."

Amen to that.

CHAPTER EIGHT

A narchy and I watched as the coffee dripped into Mr. Coffee's pot.

"It takes longer if we watch." There was a smile in Anarchy's voice.

"Sure, about that?"

"Positive." He leaned in and dropped a quick kiss on my lips. "Did you have fun last night?"

We'd come home from the party, and he'd dropped straight into bed and slept like the dead. This was our first chance to talk.

"I'm not sure fun is the right word. Everyone there quizzed me about Baxter Phelps' murder."

"Oh?" He ran his fingers through his sleep-mussed hair. It should be illegal for a man to look so appealing first thing in the morning.

"You didn't get questions?" Why was I the one inundated with demands for information? I wasn't the homicide detective.

"Ongoing investigation. I can't comment. They know that."

"Neither can I, I don't know anything."

Anarchy picked up Mr. Coffee's pot, filled my favorite mug, then pushed it toward me. I added the perfect amount of cream.

Only when I picked up the mug and sipped, did he fill his own. "Somehow, I doubt that."

I winced and took another larger sip. "Baxter Phelps met Lloyd Crowder at Nabil's the evening he died. He left the restaurant around six-thirty. He didn't return home after the meeting. At least not according to Helen."

Anarchy frowned into his coffee mug. "Lloyd didn't mention it last night."

"Your turn." Information was a two-way street.

"Phelps was killed somewhere else." Hardly breaking news. They'd opened the golf course. Only a small portion of the parking lot remained closed. If he'd been murdered at the club, everything would still be closed. "He was found at around one a.m., but we think he died around ten."

"Why Park his body in the club lot?"

"Maybe the killer wanted it found quickly."

I took a bracing sip of coffee and voiced my fear. "If the guard hadn't chased off those kids, I'd have found Baxter."

Anarchy's lips thinned. "Have you ever considered putting in a pool? I don't like you being alone at the club in the mornings."

"I don't need a pool for sunning. I need a pool for swimming. A lap pool would take up half the backyard."

"We need to find someone to go with you."

"Half the reason I swim is for the time alone. It's peaceful. No one demands a trip to the park." I nodded at the dogs, who'd already wolfed their breakfasts then returned to their beds for a bit more sleep. "No one peppers me with questions. No one insists they need new jeans right this very minute."

"Your time."

"Exactly."

"I want you to carry a gun."

"It won't do me much good in the water. Also, if it was a mob hit, there's no reason for anyone to come after me."

"You're my wife. I'm investigating." Worry added gravel to his voice.

"I'll be careful. I promise." I moseyed up to Mr. Coffee and topped of my mug. Now was my chance to tell him about the man in black. But Anarchy would worry. And we hadn't seen him at Woolf's. That he'd been at Swanson's and Harzfeld's had to be a coincidence. "So, the trunk…"

"What about it?"

"Open or cracked?"

"Cracked."

"Are you sure about that? It was Behner, the guard who found the body?"

"Yes."

"Nice man. He's good at chasing kids out of the pool. I wouldn't vouch for his observational skills. That trunk wasn't cracked. It was gaping. I'd bet on it."

A shadow passed over his features. "I'll find out."

"Also, Baxter Phelps had a gambling problem."

My husband's brows lifted. High. "That's news."

"Right? I've never heard a whisper till yesterday."

"And I thought people avoided speaking ill of the dead."

"Ha." How many times had I heard someone say, *I hate to speak ill of the dead, but Tom or Dick or Harry was a dirty dog. I hate to speak ill of the dead, but Jane or Mary or Carol was a terrible boozehound. She can't be that sad, I hate to speak ill of the dead, but her mother was a controlling witch.* That one I'd heard at a recent funeral.

He rubbed the back of his neck, then shook his head. "They circled the wagons."

I tilted chin and stared up at him. "What do you mean?"

Anarchy leaned against the counter and crossed both his arms and his ankles, his expression pensive. "Members of your set protect each other."

"Until they shove someone under an oncoming bus."

Because that's exactly what Grant had done. "I bet Perry tells you all about the gambling when you see him on Monday. According to Grant Wilcox, the house is in Helen's name so Baxter couldn't borrow against it. Maybe he borrowed money from the mob."

Anarchy tapped his index fingers against his lips, a considering look on his handsome face. "Could be. Having a tax lawyer in their debt would be…helpful. Desperate men do desperate things."

I lifted my brows and waited for more.

"Maybe Phelps helped the mob launder money."

I envisioned bills hanging on a clothesline.

He grinned as if he could read my mind. "Imagine you have a high-volume cash business. And imagine that your business is illegal—drugs or prostitution or gambling. You make money hand over fist, but you can't put the cash in the bank. If you do, the IRS may ask where it came from. You need it laundered."

"How?"

"You buy businesses that deal in cash—restaurants, paid parking lots, laundromats, bars." He winced, then added, "Strip clubs."

"Okay…"

"Those businesses report more profit than they make. The money is taxable. Clean. Laundered."

"And you think Baxter Phelps helped them do that?"

"If he owed them money?" Anarchy gave a sharp nod. "I think it's possible. I've been busy going through Baxter Phillips' case files. Maybe I should have talked to Phelps' friends. What else did you learn?"

I shook my head. "It's your turn."

He grinned. "I just told you how to launder money."

"Fascinating, but not a pertinent fact."

"We're waiting on ballistics."

"Who does the car belong to?"

"It's registered to Baxter." His gaze shifted to the window outside.

"What aren't you telling me?" I waited, willing to pout to get an answer from him.

"Baxter's body was soaked with gasoline."

"But not burned."

"No."

"Why not?"

"The killer forgot his lighter?"

He'd told me something real. It was my turn. "Whatever Baxter and Lloyd discussed when they met at Nabil's is privileged. Either they shared a client, which is doubtful since they're at different firms, or one hired the other."

Anarchy, who'd been reaching for the coffee pot, froze. "What kind of law does Crowder practice?"

"He's a corporate defense attorney, but I think he's represented corporate executives in criminal court."

"Does he take individual clients?"

"You'd have to ask him." I shrugged my shoulders. "That's all I've got."

He grinned and filled his cup. "You are truly amazing."

I felt my cheeks warm. "I try."

He put his cup on the counter and pulled me close.

I rested my free hand on his hard chest and stared up into his coffee-colored eyes.

"Think you can put that mug down?"

I wrinkled my nose. "Give up my coffee?"

"I'll make it up to you."

"Promise?"

His lips were a mere whisper from mine when Libba bellowed, "Ellison, where are you?"

Anarchy's frustrated sigh rumbled through me. "What does she want?"

"She needs to talk."

He glanced at the kitchen clock. "It's not even eight-thirty. Also, why does she still have a key?"

I ignored his question. It would be easier to put Nixon back in office than reclaim that key. "Charlie wants to get married."

He winced. "Poor guy."

I frowned, wagged my finger in his face and whispered, "nice." Then, I called, "Kitchen."

"That's my cue." He headed up the backstairs seconds before Libba burst into the kitchen.

"Coffee?" I asked.

"Please." Libba's hair was scraped back in a ponytail and her face was free of make-up. She wore a scoop-necked tee-shirt and a faded pair of jeans. In short, nothing like her usual self.

I poured her a mug and asked, "How did he propose?"

"Over dinner at The American." The American was a gorgeous restaurant at Crown Center.

I glanced at her bare left hand. "Pretty ring?"

"Gorgeous ring. Huge." An avaricious smile curled her lips and her gaze grew distant. "Huge."

"You're not marrying the ring."

"I know that," she snapped.

Did she? "Why not marry Charlie?"

She screwed her eyes shut and scrunched her pretty face. "Look around. How many of our friends are truly happy in their marriages?"

"I am."

Libba opened her eyes and fixed me with a gimlet stare. "You don't count. You spent fifteen-plus miserable years before you married Anarchy."

I couldn't argue that.

"What's to say you and Anarchy won't be miserable a decade from now?"

That I could argue. "We'll be happy."

She pursed her lips and shook her head. "How can you know that?"

"You've read those cute articles in the paper where the reporter interviews a couple who's been married for sixty years?"

"I've seen them," she allowed.

"They attribute their long marriages to not going to bed mad or making each other laugh." I shook my head. "Every day, I choose to focus on the things that make me happy—the color of Anarchy's eyes, his smile, his kiss. How he listens to me. My thoughts. My opinions."

"You mean how he lets you meddle in murder investigations."

Well, yes. Not that I'd admit that to Libba. "He's honorable, a straight arrow—"

Libba snorted, then held up her hands in apology. "Sorry, it's just that Henry was so bent, it's no wonder you picked a rule-follower for your second marriage."

"My point is this—if I obsessed over missed dinners or the way he runs toward danger, I'd be miserable in no time. I choose to focus on what makes me happy. What do you love about Charlie?"

"He's smart. He's funny. He's good in bed."

"Libba!"

"Oh, please. I bet Anarchy curls your toes."

He did. "Stop."

"Fine," she huffed. "Be a prude."

Libba, who'd been so desperate to talk she showed up before nine, was dancing around a truth she didn't want to face, deflecting with talk of my sex life.

"We're talking about you and Charlie."

She stared into her coffee cup, swirling the contents as if she could divine untold wisdom in the brown depths. I'd stared into my share of coffee cups, there were no answers there.

"What don't you love?" I asked.

"His ex-wife, his crazy hours, the way he fusses about a properly mixed Manhattan."

"And?"

"And nothing."

"Oh, please. Our mothers let us share cribs. I've known you my whole life. You don't think I can tell when there's something else?"

She flashed me a tight grin. "My crib was nicer."

"So was your mother. What else?"

Long seconds passed before she said, "I'm scared."

"Of what?"

"It's not like my parents had a happy marriage." Libba's father had ruled with an iron fist while his wife and daughter bent over backward to keep him happy. She rubbed at her eyes. "I don't want to lose myself. I can't be one of those women who puts her husband first just because he's the man."

As girls, we'd been raised to marry. Frankly, it was a miracle Libba never fell into line. As young wives (or middle-aged wives or old wives), our job was to create and maintain a happy home. That meant keeping our husbands happy. As payment, we received love (hopefully) and security. The women in my set were lucky, in addition to security, they got perks—country clubs and vacations and charge accounts at Swanson's and Woolf Brothers. "What if Charlie puts you first?"

"He's a doctor. A heart patient in crisis will always be more important than dinner with me. He's a father with children who desperately want his attention. I'll never be first."

"Have you talked to him about this?"

"No."

"Maybe you should." I kept my voice mild.

"And say what? Put me above dying patients and your children?"

"How about telling him that if you're going to make him the center of your life, you need to be the center of his?"

She scowled at me.

"What?"

"That's a very reasonable thing to say."

"It is."

"He'll know I didn't come up with it."

"Try it anyway."

She nodded. Slowly. But shadows still lingered in her eyes, and I couldn't help wondering if she'd told me everything.

CHAPTER NINE

I pulled into the Winfields'—now Millers'—circle drive, put the car in park, and waited for the valet.

A handsome young man in black pants and a black rain slicker opened my door, extending a golf umbrella over the space next to the door. "May I escort you inside, ma'am?"

Ma'am. When had I aged into being a ma'am? I swallowed a sigh and replied, "Yes, please."

With the umbrella positioned so that not a single drop of rain touched me, he escorted me to the open front door where a woman in a maid's uniform waited to take my coat.

"May I get your name, please?" asked the valet.

"Jones."

"Just let us know when you'd like your car, Mrs. Jones." He offered a brief smile, then headed back outside into the wet weather as I surrendered my raincoat.

The maid folded my bone-dry coat over her arm. "Everyone is gathering in the living room, Mrs. Jones."

"Thank you." I took a moment to catalog the changes in the house. The spacious foyer looked much as it always had—the pecan paneling had been cleaned and oiled and the floors had been refinished in a deep, rich brown. My heels sank into a pink and cream Aubusson carpet on which a gilt table held an arrangement of orchids, lilies and roses. The perfumed air smelled...expensive.

Smoothing my skirt, I stepped into a living room already half-filled with ladies dressed to the nines.

French antiques. Museum-quality French antiques. Another cream-hued Aubusson. Scalamandré fabric for the drapes. My gaze caught on the one woman I didn't recognize, and I strode toward her, extending my hand. "You must be Donna. I'm Ellison Jones. Thank you for welcoming us to your home. We've all been dying to see what you've done with the house."

Donna Miller wore Chanel. And pearls. Lots and lots of pearls. Diamond studs sparkled in her ears, and (I couldn't help but look) a diamond roughly the size of a piece of Bazooka bubble gum weighed down her ring finger. Her hair was a perfect, not-a-strand-out-of-place, honey-blonde helmet. A woman that perfect had something to prove. Either Donna Miller had married up or her husband had hit it big. I was guessing the former.

"You're the artist? I've heard so much about you." That could mean my paintings or my propensity for finding bodies. "Marilyn says you're incredibly talented. I'd love to see your work."

"Of course. We'll set up a time. What you've done with the living room is fabulous." Her decorator had mixed the French antiques with a few more modern pieces, and the drapes were lime green. The effect was elegant, unexpected and...funky (in a good way). I nodded at the window treatments. "Scalamandré?"

She nodded. "You have a good eye."

"I was hired to design a few fabrics. I looked at other design-ers." And how much they charged per yard. Donna Miller's drapes had cost a small fortune.

"I understand you're married to a homicide detective."

Had Donna memorized details about each of her guests? To be fair, Anarchy's job was more memorable than most. He wasn't just another lawyer or accountant or doctor.

"Ellison, I see you've met Donna." Marilyn joined us.

I couldn't help noticing that Marilyn's welcoming smile looked forced. "I was just admiring what Donna has done with the living room."

"You should see the kitchen." Marilyn winced. "Well, not today. Her chef and his helpers are taking up every inch. Trust me when I tell you, it's gorgeous."

"I have no doubt."

Donna smiled at me, obviously pleased. "You'll have to come for a tour."

"I'll take you up on that. What's your favorite room?"

"I'm quite fond of the conservatory. We did extensive work, added more space—more windows. It almost feels as if we're outside. Well, not that we'd want to be outside today. Such a shame about the weather. That's where we're serving luncheon."

"Donna and her husband extended the conservatory so that it spans the back of the house. There's room to seat five tables of eight."

"I can't wait to see it."

"Your table assignment is on the console." Donna nodded toward a long table topped with two Ming vases that had been converted to lamps. Neat rows of creamy card stock (folded and calligraphed) waited to be claimed. "My stars! You don't have a drink. You must think I'm a terrible hostess. What may we get you? Champagne? A mimosa? Wine?"

"I see the bar." Chester stood behind it. "And I've been monopolizing the hostess. I'll help myself." I retreated a step. "It was lovely to meet you."

"Likewise."

I ordered a seltzer and lime from Chester. When I turned, Prudence Davies stood behind me.

We regarded each other with distaste, but I took the high road. "Prudence, what a pretty dress." Maybe not so high.

She narrowed her eyes as if she sensed an insult but couldn't quite identify it. "Ellison. I heard you found another body."

"You heard wrong." No one, absolutely no one, was claiming I'd found Baxter's body. Prudence was trying to annoy me. And she was succeeding. I gritted my teeth and said a silent prayer— *please, please, please let us be seated at different tables.* I couldn't tolerate Prudence for three courses (and everything about Donna Miller and her home screamed at least three courses —four if she served an *amuse bouche* before the salad course). I eased away from Prudence, suddenly eager to check the seating assignments.

She stopped me with a taloned hand on my arm.

I stared at her fingers, with my upper lip curled, until she let me go. "What do you want, Prudence?"

"Baxter Phelps and I had mutual friends."

I stared at her. She needed to give me more than that.

She huffed as if I was an idiot, then whispered, "Mistress K."

I gaped at her. "Baxter Phelps? Boring Baxter Phelps went to Club K?" I'd discovered the club's existence when trying to prove myself innocent of my husband's murder.

"That's your problem. You never look beneath the surface."

"I don't care to speculate about other people's sex lives."

"Perhaps you should. Or your husband should."

I suppressed (barely) the urge to slap her.

She smirked as if she knew she'd gotten under my skin, that my hand itched to meet her overly rouged cheek. I'd never cause a scene like that, and she knew it.

Bad enough that I got to go home and tell my husband to go to a sex club. And not just any sex club. A *kinky* sex club—one with strange apparatus and an owner who over-filled her leather bustier. "Why are you telling me this?" In general, Prudence was the opposite of helpful.

"There you are!" Libba's hand circled my wrist as she jerked me away from the conversation with Prudence. She didn't stop jerking until we were halfway across the room. "You're welcome."

"Thank you." Not really. For once, I'd wanted to hear what Prudence had to say. The way Prudence was glaring at me from her spot near the bar (narrowed eyes, lips drawn back from her horse teeth, an ugly flush on her cheeks) suggested I'd permanently missed my chance for more information.

Libba tsked. "How did she get her hooks into you?"

"Surprise attack."

"I checked the seating. We're at table three."

"Where is Prudence?" Marilyn knew not to seat me with Prudence, but what if Donna had made the seating chart?

"Six. Wait till you see the tables."

It was a luncheon, how surprising could they be? "Why?"

She leaned close and whispered, "They're set with Royal Danica. Someone has something to prove." Royal Danica china was expensive. Very expensive. A dinner plate cost as much as a small car. It was china made for royalty (each hand-painted piece was based on a service that had been in the Dutch royal family for generations). Royalty, very old money, or very new money.

"I met Donna. She seemed nice."

"Ask Frances about Royal Danica, see what she says."

Mother would say that using china that needed to be insured to make an impression was pretentious. I didn't disagree.

When the living room was full, Marilyn tapped a silver spoon against her Champagne flute. Heads turned, and she smiled at her guests. Again, I thought her smile looked tight. Something was definitely bothering her. "I'm so glad you could join us on this rainy Monday. If you haven't yet met Donna, please introduce yourself. I know she's intimidatingly perfect, but she's actually quite nice."

The ladies in the living room tittered.

"Now, if you haven't found your table assignment, they're on the console. Please be seated. Donna has a delicious lunch planned for us."

Libba and I made our way to table three and chose seats next to each other. The table was covered with a white damask cloth and a silver Revere bowl filled with flowers sat at its center.

"Did you notice who else is sitting with us?" I asked.

"Me." Jinx looked down at the *amuse bouche* (I'd been right —four courses), and a furrow formed between her brows. "Is that—"

"Royal Danica?" Libba replied. "It is."

Jinx gave a wry laugh. "In case we missed the fortune they've spent on this place."

"Stop," I told them. "Someone will hear you." Even if our hostess was aspirational, it didn't do any good to point it out as we were sitting down to eat her food.

Jinx shrugged and eyed the baby artichoke heart filled with what looked like shrimp salad. "Who's catering?"

"Apparently, she has a chef."

"On staff? My point is made."

I hadn't cooked a meal since Aggie arrived at our home (for which the whole family was eternally grateful—no one wanted me in the kitchen). As such, I couldn't throw stones at Donna for employing a chef. Although, there was a difference. Aggie was a marvelous cook, but she was also family. How many uniformed maids did Donna employ? What would she think of my house-keeper and her exuberant kaftans? I couldn't help but smile. I'd rather have one funny, wily, loud, loyal Aggie than an army of staff. I doubted Donna would agree.

"Marilyn told me our hostess moved here from Ohio." Libba brought her water goblet to her lips and sipped.

"Akron?" My sister and her family lived in Akron.

"Toledo."

"Marilyn told you Ohio?" Jinx's perfectly arched brows lifted. "I heard New Jersey. What else did Marilyn tell you?"

Libba leaned in and whispered, "You mean where does the money come from? She didn't say, but we're scheduled for a casual lunch tomorrow."

"You'll let me know?" Jinx asked.

"I have to say, with the exception of our hostess, I'm getting old money vibes." Libba's gaze fell to the appetizer plate that could fund a nice vacation. "The china. The antiques. Ellison, what do you think of the art?"

"There are two paintings by Raoul Dufy in the living room."

"Meaning?" Libba sounded impatient.

"You're probably right. I adore his work, but he's not someone you brag about, not like Matisse or Kees Van Dongen."

"Who?"

"Other Fauvists. Never mind."

Jinx picked her crystal water goblet and took a sip. "Their son moved to Kansas City for a job—that mutual fund company on the Plaza, that's where he met Emma. I wonder what Marilyn thinks of all this." Her gaze took in the expanded conservatory, the expensive china, and the promise of a four-course lunch. "She's not one for putting on the dog."

Marilyn spent much of her time at the stable and her garden. She frequently smelled like a horse, and I'd noticed dirt beneath her fingernails more than once. She might be wearing a lovely suit today, but she'd be more comfortable in riding breeches or a pair of Bermuda shorts.

"She'd better get used to it," said Libba. "We'll all be getting a call for an impromptu engagement party later this week. Shall we entertain for Emma?" She meant hosting a shower.

"Yes," I replied as Jinx nodded. "Something at the club?"

Libba wagged her index finger at me. "Boring."

"You have a better idea?"

"We rent out a BBQ joint for an evening, hire a country band."

"That's a good idea."

"I know. Bonus, imagine Donna Miller trying to eat a rib."

"I'm sold." Jinx turned toward me. "Tell me, Ellison. What's new with Anarchy's investigation?"

CHAPTER TEN

K ey in one hand, umbrella in the other, I hurried to the front door.

It swung open before I had a chance to slip my housekey into the lock.

Aggie, who wore a Pucci-esque kaftan in shades of lemon yellow and hot pink (not the best choice with her orange hair, but she pulled it off) and giant hoop earrings, frowned at me.

"What's wrong?" I stepped inside out of the steady, warm rain.

Aggie claimed my wet umbrella. "Your mother has called five times."

Mother. Mother and Daddy were at the cottage in Michigan. "Sorry." Frankly, I'd expected a call yesterday, but news of Baxter's death had taken its sweet time traveling from Kansas City to Harbor Point. "I'll call her now."

"Thank you. Coffee?"

I glanced at my wristwatch. Nearly three o'clock. "How unhappy is she?"

Aggie scrunched her face into a sympathetic moue. "Scale of one to ten? An eleven."

Oh, dear Lord. "Perhaps a glass of wine. Are Grace or Beau at home?"

"Grace is at Peggy's. Bobby's mother called and said she'd drop him off around four."

"Good." I knew why Mother was upset, and her voice carried, even through a phone line. The children didn't need to worry about Anarchy investigating the mob. "I'll call Mother from the den." Buying myself a last moment of peace, I leaned down and scratched behind Max's velvety ears. He'd been nudging me since I walked through the door, and I was grateful for a reason to postpone calling Mother.

Max leaned into my legs and his stubby tail wagged as if it would never get another chance. "Good dog." Then, it was Finn's turn.

Too soon, the dogs left me to see what Aggie was doing in the kitchen (she might open the refrigerator without their supervision).

I gathered my courage, trudged to the family room, settled behind my desk, took a fortifying breath, and dialed.

"Walford residence." Mother's voice was cool, clipped, polished.

"It's me."

"Where have you been?"

"A luncheon at the Winfields'—well, the Millers' now."

"Until three o'clock?"

"Four courses.

"Hmph."

"Luncheon was served on Royal Danica."

Mother's answering silence spoke volumes.

"There were forty women there."

She silently tallied the cost for forty place settings of Royal Danica. "What did they serve?"

"A baby artichoke heart filled with shrimp salad, chilled asparagus soup, lobster tails, and limes filled with lime sorbet."

Mother sniffed. "Lobster for forty? Someone wants to get noticed. Who are these people?"

"Donna and Morton Miller."

"Never heard of them."

"They recently moved here. She did a beautiful job with the house." I offered Aggie a grateful smile as she placed a glass of wine on my desk.

"Be that as it may, Royal Danica and lobster?" She tsked. "This is not why I called."

I tensed. The hammer was about to fall. I lifted the wine glass to my lips.

"Baxter Phelps."

"I did not find him." I still wondered why his body had been left at the club.

"I didn't say you did." Mother sounded affronted. Nothing new. "Was he killed by the mob?"

"Maybe."

"Why is Anarchy investigating?"

"His captain assigned him the case."

"You told me there was a mob task force."

"The homicide detectives assigned to the task force are on vacation."

"I don't like it."

In that we were in complete agreement. "Neither do I."

"Tell him to drop the case."

"Anarchy doesn't get to pick his assignments."

"This is too dangerous, Ellison. It's the mob. What if they come after you or Grace or Beau?" The newest addition to our family was winning her over, a month ago she wouldn't have included him in her worry list. "Your husband needs to find a new job. I'm sure one of your father's friends would hire him." Mother would be much happier if Anarchy ran a business or a bank or, failing that, sold widgets.

"Anarchy likes his job."

"Even if it puts his family at risk?"

"We're fine. We're safe. We're—"

"I have an emergency breakthrough from Grace Russell." The operator's voice came as a shock, and I clutched the receiver so hard my hand ached.

"See? Grace has an emergency."

"Mother, I'll call you back. Thank you, operator. Hanging up now."

Seconds later, the phone rang, and I snatched the receiver from the cradle. "Grace?"

"He's outside, Mom." Her voice shook.

"Who? Where are you?"

"The man from Harzfeld's. He's standing across the street, watching Peggy's house."

My stomach flipped, then dropped to my toes, and Donna Miller's four-course lunch threatened a reappearance. "Is Peggy's mother home?"

"No."

Grace was in danger. Real danger. "Are the doors locked?"

"I don't know."

"Lock the doors. Stay in the house." I forced a calmness I didn't feel. Grace didn't need my panic. She needed a plan. "The police will be there in five minutes. I'll call them now. Do not, for any reason, leave that house."

"Okay."

I hung up and dialed Anarchy's number. My heart, which had risen to my throat, beat so hard it was difficult to breathe.

"Jones."

"Grace is in trouble."

"Where?"

I rattled off Peggy's parent's address.

"What's wrong?"

"There's a man outside the house. He followed us on the Plaza."

"A squad car is on its way. I'll be there in ten minutes."

I could be there in three.

Anarchy hung up, and I raced upstairs to my bedroom, yanked open the drawer to my bedside table, and grabbed my gun. Then I flew down the stairs and rushed to the car.

Four blocks.

Four endless blocks speeding down rain-soaked side streets. My back tires spun as I turned too fast into Peggy's driveway. Only when my car was parked behind Grace's did I look for the man in black.

There. Across the street. Exactly as Grace had described.

Water ran off a black raincoat, and his dark eyes watched as I climbed out of the car, widening when he noticed the small revolver I held next to my thigh. "Tell your husband to stop digging." His voice held a hint of New York, maybe New Jersey. "We didn't kill Phelps. We don't drop bodies at country clubs."

"Why are you stalking my daughter?" My voice was reedy, too high. Rain plastered my hair to my head and ruined my silk dress.

He shook his head, approached a dark sedan parked at the curb, opening the passenger door. "Tell him."

I shuddered at the threat in his voice.

The sedan disappeared around the corner as I heard the first police sirens.

I didn't budge until the patrol car squealed into the drive.

"Mrs. Jones?"

I recognized the officer but couldn't think of his name. "He's gone. You missed him." Not that I cared, not as long as Grace was safe.

The officer's gaze was fixed on the gun clutched in my hand.

"Sorry. I'll put this in the car." The driver's side door still stood open, and I leaned in and stashed the firearm in the glovebox.

With the gun put away, he asked, "Tell me what happened."

"Can we wait for Anarchy? I want to check on Grace." As I spoke, the front door opened, and I caught sight of Grace's face. She looked pale beneath her tan.

"Mom!" She ran outside, getting just as drenched as I was.

I wrapped her in my arms and squeezed tightly. "He's gone."

"I was so scared."

I rubbed a circle on her back. "I know, honey. But he's gone. Anarchy and I will keep you safe. I promise."

"How? It's the mob." She spoke into my shoulder.

I latched onto the first solution that came to mind. "How would you feel about a trip to Colorado?"

Grace lifted her head. "Aunt Sis?" My aunt and her new husband had a place in Vail.

"Yes. We can put you and Beau on a plane tonight." Fortunately, there were regular flights between Kansas City and Denver. "Sis will pick you up at the airport."

She stiffened, then dropped her arms and took a step backward. "What about you?"

"I'm staying here."

"But—"

"I'll be fine. Anarchy will have a squad car parked outside the house."

Her worried eyes searched my face. "Then why can't we stay?"

I managed what I hoped was a reassuring smile. "Do you want to spend the last days of summer languishing at home?" When her fear dissipated, she'd get cabin fever. And Grace with cabin fever was not fun. "You know Sis. She'll take you shopping in Denver. The house is gorgeous. You can hike and swim and go kayaking."

"But—"

"Grace, Anarchy needs to catch whoever killed that man. He has a better chance of doing that if he's not worried about your safety."

She nodded slowly. Grudgingly. "Promise you'll bring us home the minute the killer is caught."

"I promise."

Anarchy's car barreled into the drive, and he leapt from the driver's seat as the vehicle came to a stop. A second later, Grace and I were wrapped in his arms. "You're okay?"

"We're fine."

He gazed at me over her shoulder. "We need to talk."

ANARCHY HADN'T SAID TWO WORDS SINCE WE DROPPED THE KIDS off at the airport. Maybe he was mad at me. I hadn't told him about the man in black. In my defense, I never dreamed that a man I saw briefly on the Plaza would follow Grace. My defense was sound. Regardless, his angry silence made me twitchy.

I saved my anger for the man in black. He'd frightened Grace. And me. Then threatened my family. Rage burned bright in my chest, knocking elbows with regret and worry.

I already missed my children. The house felt empty without them. I dropped my handbag on the kitchen counter and opened the backdoor.

Max and Finn dashed outside, and I sighed as they ran toward the back fence line.

"I can put you on the next flight," Anarchy offered. The kids were already in the air. Aunt Sis had promised to call the moment she picked them up at the airport. Their flight had taken off just after eight, that meant we could expect a call around ten. They'd spend the night in Denver and leave for Vail in the morning. Grace and Beau would be safe.

"I'm not leaving you."

"Your mother—"

"Will have a faunching fit." I hadn't yet gathered the courage to call and tell her we'd sent the kids to Aunt Sis.

She'd be furious that I sent them to Colorado not Michigan. I already had an answer prepared. The drive from Vail to Denver was less than two hours—an easy pickup. It took more than four hours to travel from Harbor Point to Detroit. She'd be even more furious that Anarchy's job had put Grace at risk. Nor would she be happy with my decision to remain in Kansas City. She'd tell me my place was with my children. Part of me agreed with her. But Grace and Beau were safe, and Anarchy needed me (or I needed him). I cringed in anticipation of the vitriol coming my way. "I don't care what Mother says. I'm not leaving you."

He rubbed a hand across his stubbled chin. "Do you want a drink?"

"Please."

"Vodka, gin, wine?"

Was one of each an option? "Wine. A small one." If the mob was lurking, letting alcohol impair my judgment was foolish.

"I'll meet you in the den."

A moment later, he joined me on the couch where I'd curled into the corner. I broke off staring at the dark television screen to accept the wine glass he offered. "Thank you."

"You're welcome. Now, tell me."

I took a sip first. The wine was cold and crisp and much needed. "I saw him at Harzfeld's when Grace and I went shopping. Grace said she'd noticed him at Swanson's. When we took our bags to the car, I felt like someone was watching us."

"You didn't mention it." He sounded almost...flinty.

"It's not unusual to see the same people at both stores. It could have been a coincidence, and I didn't want to worry you."

Anarchy rested his head against the back of the couch and stared at the ceiling. His lips moved as if he was silently begging for patience or wisdom or the right words to tell me how stupid I'd been. "I never imagined the mob would target our family. I'm sorry."

"It's not your fault." I tucked my left foot beneath me. "When I saw him at Peggy's house my heart stopped."

"What were you thinking? Going there alone?" His voice was too sharp.

I blinked back the sudden urge to cry. "I was thinking Grace was in danger."

"Going put you both in danger."

"In my place, what would you have done?" We both knew, he'd have done the same darned thing. "He said they didn't kill Baxter."

"Right. I hear the dogs." He rose from the couch and disappeared into the kitchen.

I heard the backdoor open, and a moment later, the dogs raced into the family room.

"Ugh. You're wet." Dampness soaked their paws, and Finn jumped on the couch as if we allowed dogs on the furniture. "Off!"

He grinned at me and wagged his tail.

I gave him a gentle shove, and he landed on the floor, still grinning.

"You need a walk." Where would I find the energy? Worry and anger and sadness seemed to have seeped into my bones, leaving me unwilling to leave the comforts of my couch.

Anarchy stood in the room's entrance with his arms crossed over his chest. "Not tonight they don't. Tomorrow, we'll hire someone, or Aggie can take them. You are not walking around the neighborhood unprotected."

Max was excellent protection, but I didn't argue the point. Not even my fearless Weimaraner could protect me from a bullet. "Look, I know you're mad at me, but—"

"Mad at you? My job put Grace at risk. You're the one who should be mad." Anarchy sank onto the couch. He'd returned from the kitchen with a finger of scotch in an old-fashioned glass and he took a sip.

"It's not your fault."

"It is." He stared at the drink in his hands.

"I could have told you about the man in black."

He dismissed my point with a quick shake of his head. "This one's on me, and I'm so, so sorry."

"How about we both stop blaming ourselves? Grace is fine. She and Beau are safe. Nothing happened."

He shifted his gaze from the scotch to me, and he nodded.

"You still think the mob killed the wrong Baxter?" I asked.

"Seems that way. Especially now that their threatening my family."

I screwed my eyes shut, the brief scene with the man in black playing against my eyelids. "It's the oddest thing, but I believed him. What if he was telling the truth?"

"Ellison—"

"I mean it. Prudence told me that Baxter frequented Club K—"

"You told me he was boring."

"That was before I knew about the gambling and the sex. Apparently, I didn't know him very well."

Anarchy's laugh held a bitter edge.

I tucked my left leg beneath me and took another sip of wine. "They want you to stop digging. What are you digging?"

"Baxter Phillips is prosecuting a low-level made guy. I'm trying to figure out why they'd risk killing a prosecutor over Nico Rossi."

"Maybe—"

"No, Ellison. It's the mob. They killed the wrong guy."

"So, you're going to keep digging." It wasn't a question. And I wasn't convinced that he was on the right trail.

Anarchy clinked the ice in his scotch. "Yes."

"Promise me you'll be careful."

"If you'll promise the same."

"Done."

"The patrol officer said you had a gun with you."

My shoulders stiffened, readying for a lecture. "I did."

"Good. Don't leave the house without it."

CHAPTER ELEVEN

P er Anarchy's request, I'd skipped my morning swim and asked Aggie to walk the dogs. No kids. No dogs. No Aggie. No Anarchy (he'd left early for work). Just me and Mr. Coffee. Good thing he was excellent company.

I topped off my mug. "What if Anarchy's wrong about the mob?"

Why would someone kill Baxter?

"I don't know," I groaned. "I wish I knew what he and Lloyd Crowder discussed the night Baxter died. Then there's the gambling…and the sex."

The sex? If Mr. Coffee had eyebrows, they'd be at the lid I lifted when I added water.

"I forgot to tell you. Prudence Davies says that Baxter frequented Club K."

Wow.

I took a sip of coffee "Right?"

Did his wife know?

I remembered Helen's reddened eyes and shaking fingers. "I don't think so."

So, where's the motive?

"Maybe he saw someone at the club."

Seems like the people in that lifestyle protect each other's privacy.

I didn't question how my coffeemaker knew that. I wasn't sure I wanted the answer. "I should find out if Baxter had a regular partner at Club K."

How?

"I could go to the club."

Do you think the owner will tell you?

"There's only one way to find out."

What will Anarchy say?

"He's busy following the mob angle. If I find anything, I'll tell him."

If you don't find anything?

Ugh. I stared into my coffee mug.

Ask for forgiveness rather than permission?

"Permission? I don't need my husband's permission to a sex club."

Mr. Coffee chuckled. *You may want to rethink that statement.*

A YOUNG MAN WEARING LEATHER PANTS AND A DOG COLLAR opened the door at Club K. No shirt. And, dear, God, he'd pierced his nipples. That had to hurt.

I forced my gaze to his face. "I'd like to speak with Kathleen Mahoney."

"Who?" He looked genuinely confused.

"Mistress K."

"Are you interested in a membership?" His kohl-lined eyes took in my khaki shirt dress and espadrilles.

"I'm interested in speaking with Ms. Mahoney." My voice came out sharper than I intended, and the young man's eyes widened as he caught his lower lip in his teeth. "You may tell her that Ellison Russell Jones is here to see her."

"Yes, ma'am." He stepped back, lowering his gaze and allowing me entrance to a place I'd hoped never to visit again. "I'm Billy." His voice had turned husky. "You can always ask for me."

Oh, dear Lord. "Ms. Mahoney?"

"Please, wait here." He hurried up a flight of stairs on the far side of the space.

The first floor of Club K was open, filled with odd apparatuses, black leather, a simple bar, and a brick wall hung with whips and floggers and crops. My skin itched with the urge to leave. Instead, I straightened my shoulders and waited.

"I didn't expect to see you again, seersucker." The dominatrix hadn't changed. Same bright red lipstick, heavy black eyeliner, and contoured cheeks. Same sleek ponytail.

A year ago, she'd made me blush. Today, any flush in my cheeks was from annoyance, not embarrassment. "Baxter Phelps."

She tilted her head. "What about him?"

"He's dead."

She blinked.

"You didn't know."

She shrugged. "Haven't seen him since Thursday."

"He was here? Thursday night?"

"You still married to a cop?"

"I am."

"Maybe I should call a lawyer."

I shrugged with feigned nonchalance. "You could do that."

"You're different." She narrowed her eyes and stroked her index finger from the tip of her nose to the point of her chin. "Your husband doesn't know you're here."

And if he found out, he wouldn't be happy. "He's pursuing other leads. How long has Baxter been a member here?"

"Three months. Maybe four. He was new to the lifestyle."

Lifestyle? I pressed my lips together, keeping my opinions to myself.

"He embraced it fully."

Bleh. "Was there anyone special with whom Baxter spent time?" Good Lord, I sounded stuffy.

A shadow crossed over Kathleen's striking face. She might be Mistress K to her clients, but I refused to think of her in those terms. "Audrey."

"Last name?"

She shook her head.

"Slender, dark hair, doe eyes?"

"You're describing Audrey Hepburn."

No. I was describing Audrey Miles, the only Audrey I'd ever actually met, a divorcée with a reputation for walking on the wild side. "Petite. Sounds breathless when she speaks."

"You know her?"

God, help me. I did. I gave a brief nod.

"Audrey and Baxter spent Monday afternoons and Thursday nights together. When she didn't show up on Thursday night, Baxter left."

"What time?"

"Seven? Eight? I couldn't say for sure."

"Did either of them spend time with anyone else?"

"Audrey did, And, no, I'm not telling you his name."

"There wasn't any jealousy?"

"Not that I know of."

"When did Audrey meet her other lover?"

"Lover? Still pure as the driven snow, aren't you?"

Kathleen Mahoney made monogamy sound dull. It wasn't. "Just answer the question." My voice was mild, as if she'd lost the ability to annoy me.

She looked slightly put out at my sangfroid. "Every other weekend."

Which made sense. Audrey and Gibson Miles were divorced. He probably took his children every other weekend. "Has Audrey been here since Thursday?"

"No. But I wasn't expecting her."

"Thank you for your time." I turned toward the door.

"Henry was wrong about you."

"My late husband was wrong about a lot of things."

"He thought you were weak."

"Like you said, he was wrong." I lifted my chin and stepped outside onto the broken sidewalk. After the dark shadows of Club K, the August sun seemed particularly bright, and I dug through my handbag for my sunglasses. Trash blew across the street, and a faded real estate sign offered buildings for sale.

"I didn't figure you went to places like this."

My head jerked up.

The man in black leaned against a sedan with his arms folded over his chest.

"You followed me." And I was alone in a district filled with neglected warehouses and empty parking lots. If I told Anarchy (when I told Anarchy), he'd point out going to Club K by myself was the opposite of being careful. And he'd be right.

"It wasn't hard. Did you give your husband our message?"

"I did." My hand, which was still in my handbag, closed around my gun, even as my heart beat triple time. "What do you want?"

"What are you doing here?"

Telling the truth seemed the wisest course. "Baxter Phelps came here on Thursday night before he was murdered."

Dark glasses hid the man-in-black's eyes, so it was hard to get a read on his expression, but I got the sense that I'd surprised him. "You interrogate your husband's suspects?"

"Kathleen Mahoney isn't a suspect."

"But you did interrogate her."

"I asked her a few questions."

"And what did she tell you?"

"That Baxter Phelps was a regular on Thursday nights. What's your name?"

His brows lifted above the rims of his sunglasses.

"You know my name..."

"Frank. My name is Frank."

"Thank you."

He inclined his head as if he'd done me a tremendous favor.

"Listen, Frank. I don't think you or your associates killed Baxter, but I need to come up with some solid leads to convince my husband of that. Scaring our daughter didn't do you any favors when it comes to believing in your innocence." My fingers felt clammy on the gun's grip.

"Gun in your purse?" Frank sounded amused.

"Yes."

"You gonna shoot me?"

"Probably not. No. Not unless you pull a gun."

"You think you're faster than me?"

"I know I am." My gun was already pointed at his chest. "And I don't miss."

He laughed, hard enough to bend him at the waist. When he straightened, he wiped a smile off his lips with an open palm. "I like you, Ellison."

I stiffened.

"What? You're using my first name."

Only because he hadn't offered his surname.

"You think you can find Phelps' killer? What does a lady like you know about murder?"

Way too much. "If I find a solid lead, my husband will follow it."

"And stay out of our business."

"Anarchy is investigating a murder. If the real killer is caught, he'll stop digging."

"Will he?"

"He will." I sound a lot more confident than I felt.

"Well, then, what's our next step?"

Wait. What? Our?

"You got a lead in there. I can tell."

"What if I did?"

"Fine. Don't tell me. I'll just follow you."

Audrey Miles frequented a sex club, that didn't mean she deserved the mob's attention. "No."

"Yes."

I could call Audrey. "I'm going home."

"Then I'll follow you there." He grinned. "Think of me as your shadow."

Oh, dear Lord. "Fine. We're going to Fairway." I circled my car, yanked open the driver's door, and climbed in. I didn't bother looking to see what Frank did. I already knew. He was following me.

The difference between the West Bottoms and Fairway, Kansas was stark. Gone were the crumbling sidewalks, moldering warehouses, and trash-lined gutters. Instead, small, manicured lawns led to neat Cape Cod style cottages. Flowers abounded, spilling from borders and pots. Oak trees offered welcome shade.

I parked at the curb in front of Audrey's house (I'd been here twice for parents' association meetings) and strode toward the front door. I felt, rather than saw, Frank park several doors down.

With my nose in the air, I ignored him and knocked. When my knuckles met the brightly painted door, it cracked open.

My stomach sank.

Then the smell hit me, and my stomach twisted with sudden nausea. I knew that smell. Death.

Still, I pushed the door open and called, "Audrey?"

No one answered.

I took a single step inside and looked to my right.

Audrey Miles's body was splayed across the Berber carpet

that covered her living room floors. The cream wool was stained a rusty brown with dried blood, and Audrey's eyes stared sightlessly at the ceiling.

Holding my breath, I hurried to the kitchen, picked up the phone, and called my husband.

"Jones."

"I'm at Audrey Miles's house. She's dead."

"Who is Audrey Miles?"

"Baxter Phelps' mistress. She's been murdered." I gave him the address.

"That's in Kansas. They'll have to request our assistance." None of the small cities that stretched along the Missouri-Kansas border employed homicide detectives. On the rare occasion a murder happened in their jurisdiction, they requested assistance from the Kansas City, Missouri police department. "You're sure it's murder?"

"There's lots of blood."

"I'll call it in."

I hung up the phone and hurried outside where I gulped huge breaths of hot, humid air. When my stomach calmed, I walked up to Frank's car and tapped on the window.

"Where to next?" he asked.

"Nowhere. She's dead. The police are on their way."

"Dead, how?"

"There's a hole in her chest."

Frank gave a short, grim nod. "I'll be seeing you." Then, he rolled up his window and drove away.

I returned to my car and tried to figure out how to tell my husband that I'd gone to a sex club without him. And that was the easy part of the conversation. How did I explain Frank?

CHAPTER TWELVE

T he police arrived, took a brief statement, and told me to go home.

I was only too happy to comply, but I waited for Anarchy instead. An enormous oak offered me shade, and I lingered beneath its branches pondering how in the world I could explain what brought me to Audrey's house.

When he arrived, he strode toward me with a thunderous expression on his lean face. His hands closed around my upper arms, and his coffee-brown eyes searched mine. "You're okay?"

"Fine." I jerked my head toward the house. "It's bad." Thank heavens I'd found Audrey. Seeing their mother's body like that would have scarred her children forever. "There's a lot of blood."

"Phelps' mistress?"

I wrinkled my nose.

"What?" he demanded.

"They were definitely having sex, but I'm not sure 'mistress' is the right term."

"Jones." Peters, Anarchy's irascible partner, glared at me from Audrey's front stoop as if I were responsible for delaying his investigation.

"Coming." Again, Anarchy's gaze searched my face. He knew there was something I wasn't telling him. With a discontented huff, he said, "I'll see you at home."

"I'll be there."

Driving home, I couldn't help but check the rearview mirror to see if Frank was following me. If he was, I couldn't spot him.

I parked in the circle drive in front of the house and took a moment to think. A sex club, an unexplainable alliance with a member of the mafia, and now I'd found a body—and I'd only told my husband about one of those things.

He wasn't thrilled about the body.

He'd be even less thrilled about the other two.

I tightened my grip on the wheel and stared at my hostas as if their green leaves could save me.

A tap on the passenger-side window startled me out of my skin. When my poor, abused heart returned to my chest, I snapped, "What?"

"Sorry." Aggie held up her hands in apology. "Marilyn Tremblay is on the phone. She says it's important."

I had a decent excuse for being short. Decent, not good. "I found a body, and it's put me out of sorts. I'm sorry for snapping at you."

Aggie waved away my apology. "My fault for sneaking up on you. Who died?"

"Audrey Miles."

"Should I bake a Bundt?"

"Probably." Then I added, "She was murdered."

Aggie nodded as if she'd expected nothing less. "Do you want to talk about it?"

The blood, the smell—I couldn't talk about it. Not yet. "No, but thank you for offering."

I climbed out of the car and headed inside. The dogs greeted me with wagging tails and hopeful expressions. "Give me a minute," I told them as I walked into the kitchen and picked up the receiver. "Hello, Marilyn."

"Ellison, I hope I didn't catch you at a bad time."

"Not at all," I lied.

"Morton Miller's mother has decided to come to Kansas City."

Bully for her. "Oh?"

"She hates to fly—absolutely loathes being in the air. She leaves Boston the day after Thanksgiving and flies to Palm Beach. She stays there till mid-April. Two flights a year. The fact that she's coming to Kansas City is a big deal. She wants to meet you."

There was still coffee in Mr. Coffee's pot. How long had it been there? Could I pour it over ice?

"She has one of your paintings hanging in her house in Florida. Please say you'll come to the engagement party on Friday night."

There were a million reasons to stay home. Marilyn and I weren't close friends. I barely knew Emma. I'd never met the groom. I'd just found a body. Anarchy was busy with a case.

"Please." She sounded desperate. "Donna called and begged me. I guess Honoria is something of a force. They're all terrified of her. Please, Ellison. She's old Boston. A Brahmin. She already thinks we're uncultured savages. Having you there could save the evening."

I picked up Mr. Coffee's pot and swirled the contents. They looked like sludge, and with a silent sigh, I poured the coffee down the drain. "Marilyn..."

"Please? I wouldn't ask if it weren't important."

"Fine." I ceded out of exhaustion, not any desire to attend. "Where and when?"

"Donna and Morton's house at six-thirty."

"Attire?"

"Cocktail."

"The invitation includes Anarchy?" If it didn't, I'd be staying home.

"Yes, yes, of course, Anarchy is invited. Also..." she drew out the word. That couldn't be good.

"What?"

"Donna wants to see your studio."

"She mentioned something about that at the luncheon. Which was lovely, thank you for including me."

"I'm glad you enjoyed it. About Donna, she can be...a handful."

Today, I'd dealt with a dead body, the mafia, and a dominatrix, how tough could Donna be? "I'm sure I can handle her."

"It's just that she was on her best behavior on Monday." Marilyn wasn't a woman who spoke ill of others. Especially not her daughter's future mother-in-law.

"How bad is it?"

"We adore Price, but we've asked Emma to think long and hard about marrying him. His mother...let's just say I wouldn't want that woman to have any input in my life." *That woman.* That wasn't good.

"I'm here if you need to talk. And I keep my mouth shut."

"Thank you, Ellison. You're a good friend. I won't keep you." She probably had other calls to make. "We'll see you Friday."

We hung up.

Aggie, who'd entered the kitchen as Marilyn and I were saying our goodbyes, gave me an appraising look. "The body?"

"Like I said, Audrey Miles."

"A friend?"

"An acquaintance."

"You look pale. What else is wrong?"

"I went to Club K this morning."

"Club K?"

"My late husband's sex club. Baxter Phelps' sex club."

She picked up a dishcloth and wiped the already spotless counter. "I remember now. It's somewhere in the West Bottoms."

"That's right."

"Does Anarchy know?"

"I haven't had a chance to tell him yet."

"He asked you to stay safe, and you went to a sex club in the warehouse district?" Aggie grasped the problem immediately. "I see why you haven't told him."

"It gets worse. The man who followed Grace followed me. His name is Frank."

Aggie paled.

"That's not the worst part. Kathleen Mahoney, the woman who runs the club, told me who Baxter met at the club—Audrey Miles. Her murder was brutal."

"With respect to Mrs. Miles, that's not the worst part. Your husband is used to you finding bodies, but I think he'll take exception to the sex club—and to your being on a first-name basis with a made man."

She wasn't wrong. Anarchy was convinced that the mob was behind Baxter's death.

I wasn't so sure. "I don't think Frank and his associates are responsible for Baxter's death. The man was a gambler and frequented sex clubs. Seems like there might be a motive there."

"Maybe you should talk to the wife again."

"Helen?" It wasn't an excellent idea. If Baxter was cheating, she might have chosen murder over divorce. "I can't show up empty-handed."

"I made raspberry jam last week. I can put a ribbon on a jar for you."

"Thank you. What would I do without you?"

~

TEN MINUTES LATER, I WALKED UP THE FRONT PATH TO HELEN'S door, gingham-ribboned jam in hand.

"She's not home."

I looked around for the owner of the voice.

"Screened porch, dear. Come inside out of the sun." The screen door of the house next door swung open.

Some neighbors gossiped, others watched comings and goings, I had a feeling this one did both.

I cut across Helen's driveway and stepped inside her neighbor's porch. The voice's owner was a woman with white hair tied in a braid. She wore a pink housecoat edged in white rick rack and Dr. Scholl's sandals. Her face was lined with wrinkles, but her eyes glinted with intelligence. "You were here on Friday," she said. "You brought cake."

"I did."

"Sit." She waved at a wicker chair. "May I offer you tea?"

"Please."

She nodded, as if she'd expected my response. "I'm Sherry. Sherry Patterson."

"Nice to meet you, Mrs. Patter—"

"Sherry. Call me Sherry."

"Nice to meet you, Sherry. I'm Ellison Jones."

"Well, Ellison Jones, make yourself at home. I'll be back in a tick with your tea."

She disappeared into the house, and I took a moment to admire her porch. It was enormous. A jute carpet covered the floor, and Boston ferns—ten, by my count—hung from hooks on the support beams. Two white wicker chairs clustered near a wicker coffee table, and a chaise lounge with a harvest gold cushion sat in the corner. Above it all, a ceiling fan made the heat bearable.

"I can't abide air-conditioning. I spend most of my time out here." Sherry offered me a sweating glass then claimed the other chair.

"Thank you for the tea."

"I have lemon," she said, nodding to a wedge-filled dish on the coffee table. "You look like the kind of woman who takes lemon in her tea."

Not daring to argue, I squeezed a wedge. "Your porch is heavenly."

"I like it." Her satisfaction with her little oasis was evident in her voice. "I'd like it even more if the house was on the other side of the street."

"Oh?"

"Those houses have a view of the golf course. At any rate, I have no complaints. I love the fresh air and the chaise is comfortable. When it's this hot, I even sleep out here."

"I'd think it would be too loud."

She chuckled. "The locusts have been busy this year."

I glanced at the Phelps' house. "I meant the neighbors."

"Helen and Baxter? Quiet as church mice. Except for Thursdays. He's out late on Thursdays."

"Last Thursday?"

"He didn't come home."

"Did Helen leave?"

Sherry was too canny not to understand what I was asking. "You're barking up the wrong tree. Helen was home all night. I'd have heard if she started her car."

Helen had an alibi.

Whoever had killed Baxter Phelps, it wasn't his wife.

THE SHADOWS WERE LENGTHENING BY THE TIME I GOT HOME from Sherry's. I groaned when I spotted a strange Mercedes parked in the driveway. To quote Dorothy Parker, "What fresh hell was this?"

I pulled my car around to the back of the house and entered through the kitchen door.

Aggie, who stood near the sink, looked visibly relieved to see me.

"Who's here?" I asked.

Aggie leaned against the counter and closed her eyes. "She told me her name is Donna Miller. She's drinking gin in the living room. Every ten minutes, she demands to know when you'll be home."

My lips thinned. I didn't appreciate anyone putting a harried expression on Aggie's face. "I'll take care of it."

Gathering the fraying threads of my patience, I headed to the living room and found it empty. Empty except for an abandoned pair of black patent pumps.

Had she left? Could I be that lucky? Probably not without her shoes. I returned to the front hall, peeked outside, and saw her car. Next, my gaze landed on the cracked door to Anarchy's study.

Was Donna snooping? Hurrying across the foyer, I pushed open the door.

Donna stood at Anarchy's desk. She wore linen pants, a creamy silk shirt, and a shocked expression. "Ellison."

"Donna." My voice was steel. "What are you doing in here?"

"I always like to see what books people read." She waved at the bookcases. She'd have been more believable if I hadn't found her next to my husband's desk.

"There are no books on the desk." Just a file that Anarchy had brought home from the station.

She wrinkled her nose in a whoops expression.

I wasn't buying it. I opened the door wider and waved toward the foyer, a clear indication to leave the study.

She sighed as if I was imposing but followed me into the living room.

Donna claimed a wingback chair, lit a cigarette, and exhaled a stream of smoke.

I hated smoking in the house. The acrid scent would linger in the upholstery for days. Libba, who indulged in the occasional cigarette, smoked on my patio. Never inside. And she was my best friend. Why Donna Miller thought she could light up without asking my blessing was beyond me. One would think the lack of ashtrays in the living room would have hinted that smoking was unwelcome. Either she was oblivious or rude.

Rude. Definitely rude.

She tapped her ash into a silver-edged crystal coaster, and asked, "Where have you been?"

I blinked back my surprise. "Did we have an appointment?" We most definitely had not.

"You said you'd show me your studio."

I offered her a tight smile. "Now isn't the best time."

"Why not? I'm here, you're here."

"I've had a long day." An understatement. If I went to my third-floor studio, it would be to paint—not to entertain a spoiled woman who thought she could show up at my house, treat my housekeeper poorly, smoke, and make demands on my time.

She crushed her cigarette and lit another. "So, where is your studio?"

"Today isn't good for me."

"I can come back tomorrow."

Please, no. "I'd hate to waste your time."

Her eyes narrowed to slits. "What do you mean?"

"Perhaps we should chat with our calendars in front of us. Tomorrow isn't good for me." Liar, liar, pants on fire. I scratched my nose, then added, "Besides, I'm sure you'll be busy getting ready for the engagement party on Friday night."

She rolled her eyes. "The staff handles that."

Of course, they did.

I crossed the room to the library table near the front

windows, pulled a bridge pad from a drawer, and jotted down my phone number. Then I offered her the slip of paper. "Why don't you call me when you get home? We'll find a mutually convenient time."

"I still don't see why you can't do as I ask. I'm already here."

"Donna, we've only just met, so you don't know me well, but 'no' means 'no.' As I mentioned, I've had a long day. If you don't mind, I'll send you on your way."

Her mouth opened and closed as if she couldn't believe I was asking her to leave my home.

Believe it, lady.

With an offended huff, she jammed her feet in her shoes, collected her handbag, and muttered, "One would think you'd be nicer to potential clients."

For Marilyn's sake, I took the high road. "I appreciate your interest in my work but showing you my studio isn't convenient right now."

With her nose lifted high in the air, Donna strode out my front door.

I had not made a friend, and I didn't much care.

I watched until she turned out of the drive, then returned to Anarchy's office. With the tip of my finger, I flipped open the file on his desk and found a photo of Baxter's dead body.

Great. Just great. Donna had rifled through an active case file.

One more thing to confess to Anarchy. I took a calming breath—a breath completely ruined by a shuddering crash from the back of the house.

CHAPTER THIRTEEN

I ran to the kitchen to find a pan of lasagna splattered across the floor. Aggie, who was covered in tomato sauce, had a death grip on Finn's collar. She was slowly dragging the dog, whose legs were splayed, toward the back door.

I skirted the mess and opened the door for her.

She shoved him into the yard. "Bad dog!"

An unrepentant Finn tried to slip back into the house.

"No!" She wagged her finger at him. "Bad, bad dog. He tripped me."

"Max." I gave our Weimaraner the stink eye. "Out."

With poor grace, he'd happily clean the floor for us, he deigned to go outside.

"They're always underfoot."

"I know. I'm sorry."

"I don't have anything else for dinner."

"We'll go to the club." A tiny part of me was relieved. I couldn't discuss Mistress K at the country club.

"I'm so sorry about this." Aggie scowled at the messy floor.

"Not your fault. How can I help?"

"I'll take care of it. You've already had a day."

"It just keeps getting better. Donna was snooping in Anarchy's office. I think she went through his case file."

Aggie frowned. "Why would she do that?"

I had no idea. "She's nosey?"

"Will you tell Anarchy?"

"Yes." That was a conversation we could have over dinner, no matter where we were. He wouldn't be happy, but Donna's nosiness wasn't anything we could have anticipated. Who went to someone's house, snuck into the study, and read files? No one. Well, no one but Donna Miller.

"What did you learn from Helen Phelps?"

"Helen wasn't home. I visited with her next-door neighbor. Sherry's a character. She sleeps on her screened porch and keeps an eye on everyone's comings and goings. Sherry seems sure that Helen was home the night of the murder. Murders. I assume Audrey was also killed on Thursday."

Aggie fetched the dustbin and dishcloth and scooped lasagna off the floor. Suddenly, my stomach turned. The tomato sauce looked too much like blood.

"Get out of here. You look like you're gonna be sick." And she had enough to clean up.

With a palm pressed against my mouth, I did as she asked.

Two hours later, I followed the hostess at the club to a table by the window. Every table in the dining room was covered with a crisp white linen cloth, and votives flickered at their centers.

I felt other diners' stares as I walked by them. As soon as I passed, they'd be quietly speculating about Baxter's death, wondering if Anarchy was chasing a lead. Coming here had been a mistake. I should have run down to the Plaza and grabbed a hamburger from Winstead's.

"Will Mr. Jones be joining you?"

"I'm not sure." I'd left a message for him. "Perhaps a drink while I wait—a gin and tonic, please."

"Two limes?"

"Please."

"We'll have that right out for you, Mrs. Jones." It couldn't come fast enough.

She left me, and I directed my attention to the view outside. Flowers rioted in pots on the patio. Past that, the golf course looked like green velvet.

"Ellison."

I'd made it forty-five seconds before someone approached the table. I pulled my gaze from the window and found Grant Wilcox looming over me. "Good evening."

"Are you dining alone?"

"Honestly, I'm not sure."

"Your husband is still investigating Baxter's murder? Hasn't caught the killer yet?"

I wish I knew who sat on the membership committee when the Wilcoxes were invited to join the club. I had a few choice words for them.

"These things take time." Especially when a second murder complicated things. No way was I telling him about Audrey Miles. If I was lucky, no one would ever learn I found her body.

"You told him about the gambling?"

"I did."

Grant nodded sagely. "Poor Helen put up with a lot."

If he only knew. "You were the first person to mention gambling."

He shrugged. "I thought it might help catch Baxter's killer." He looked sincere in that aw-shucks way very few men over twenty could pull off. He even sounded sincere, practically dripping candor. So why didn't I believe him?

"When did he stop?"

"Pardon?" Grant rocked back on his heels and crossed his arms.

"Helen said he quit gambling. When did he stop?"

"I'm not sure he ever did. Poor Helen." His eyes crinkled with sympathy. I wasn't buying his act.

"Your drink, Mrs. Jones."

"Thank you." I lifted the glass to my lips, glad for the gin's sharp bite.

"You're sure you won't join us?"

I didn't trust Grant. He was hiding something. "You know what? I'd be delighted."

I stood, and Grant escorted me to a table in the center of the dining room. Sandy, who'd remained seated, looked up from perusing the menu. "So glad you decided to join us."

"It was kind of you to ask."

"Your menu, Mrs. Jones." The same waiter who'd brought my drink offered a menu.

"Thank you, Lenny."

Lenny gave a brief nod and left us.

"What's your usual order?" asked Sandy.

"The house salad with grilled chicken."

"That's why you girls are so thin. You eat rabbit food. You should order steak or a pork chop with a baked potato."

"I think I'll stick with the salad tonight." God, save me from men who told women what to eat.

Grant frowned and drained his scotch. Then he twisted in his chair, looking for Lenny. When he didn't immediately catch the waiter's eye, he waved. Seeing him, Lenny took a quick step toward our table, but Grant merely pointed at his empty glass.

I kept my face blank. I might judge the man with whom I was eating dinner, but I'd be damned if I'd reveal my disapproval at the table. I took a sip of my cocktail and cast about for a topic of conversation. "Do you eat here often?"

"Several nights a week. Last Thursday the chef made the most marvelous salad for me—butter lettuce, strawberries, blueberries, red onion, and goat cheese." Sandy reached over and patted her husband's hand. "And you weren't here to pressure me to eat a hamburger instead."

Something in me stilled. "Were you working?"

"Heavens, no," said Sandy. "He met Lloyd Crowder for dinner, then they met up with their cronies to play cards."

Lloyd Crowder had dined with his wife last Thursday. At Nabil's. Of that I was certain. Then, they'd gone home together. Somehow, I kept my face blank. "The salad sounds delicious. Have you talked to Helen? I went by to see her today, but she wasn't home."

"She's staying with her brother and his family for a few days. I think she's afraid to be alone in the house. I can't say as I blame her."

I stayed in my house after my husband's murder. But if I had Grace to think about it, and I'd been a suspect, I'd worried that leaving would make me look guilty. "I still can't figure out why anyone would kill Baxter."

"I told you. He had a gambling problem."

I turned to look at Grant. "If someone owed me money, I wouldn't kill him. Dead men can't repay their debts."

"I've heard it was the mob. Maybe they were making an example of him."

"To whom? It's not like the members here making a habit of doing business with the mafia."

Grant's mouth narrowed into an unhappy line. He didn't have an answer for that. "Maybe Helen killed him."

"Helen was home all night."

"According to who?" he demanded.

"Her lovely, nosey, very observant neighbor."

"Well, it's not my job to solve your husband's cases."

The hand in my lap crushed my napkin, "I'm sorry if I gave you the impression it was."

Grant looked as if he deeply regretted inviting me to join their table.

"Ellison, look. Isn't that your husband?"

I turned. Anarchy stood in the dining room entrance and scanned the tables.

I stood, and he strode toward us.

"I wasn't sure if you'd make it, and the Wilcoxes asked me to join them."

"Sandy, nice to see you again." Anarchy offered his hand, and the two shook. Then he held out his hand to Grant.

The two men clasped hands, and I got the impression that Grant's shake was stronger than it needed to be.

When they separated, Anarchy nodded to the last chair. "May I?"

"Please," Sandy replied.

Anarchy sat, taking in the nervous flutter of Sandy's hands, the dark flush on Grant's cheeks, and my death grip on my old-fashioned glass. Then, he offered us a slow grin. "How about those Royals?"

AFTER A STILTED, UNCOMFORTABLE DINNER—DURING WHICH Anarchy and Grant discussed baseball and Sandy wondered how many calories were in the salad dressing—we returned home and found a message written in Aggie's loopy handwriting: *Please call your aunt.*

A shot of pure terror stole my breath, and my heart stalled in my chest

Anarchy gave my hand a quick squeeze. "They're fine. I promise. If it was an emergency, Aggie would have called us at the club."

He was right. My head knew it. The rest of my body didn't get the memo.

It was with shaking hands that I grabbed the phone and dialed.

Aunt Sis picked up on the third ring.

"It's me."

"Oh, good! The kids want to talk to you."

My heart resumed beating.

"Grace, your mother is on the line," I heard her say in the background.

A moment later, my daughter's voice came through. "Has Anarchy caught the killer?"

"Not yet. Are you okay? Are you having fun?"

She took a breath before she replied, "Aunt Sis is great, and we love Vail, but…"

"But?"

"I want to come home." I could hear the longing in her voice. She was missing end-of-summer parties, and shopping trips with her friends.

"He's working on it, honey."

"Can he work faster?"

I laughed. I couldn't help it. "I'll tell him you asked. Is Beau around?"

"He's right here. I'll put him on."

"Beau?"

"This place is awesome! Can we come here for vacation next summer?"

"Yes, if you'd like. I'll see about renting a place over the holidays. It's been forever since I've been skiing."

Anarchy, who stood on the other side of the kitchen island, raised a brow.

"You and Anarchy can take lessons; you'll pick it up in no time. It's almost like flying. Are you getting plenty to eat?" The boy put away more food than seemed humanly possible.

"Aunt Sis is like you. She doesn't cook, so she took us out for pizza tonight. How's everything at home?"

My heart squeezed. "We're fine. Anarchy is working lots of

hours. The dogs are in trouble. Finn made Aggie drop a lasagna this afternoon."

"I bet she was mad."

"Yep." I popped the 'p.'

"I miss you."

There it was again, the squeeze around my heart. "I miss you too. We'll see you soon."

"When's soon?"

"Soon. May I talk to Aunt Sis?"

"Yeah." He sounded so disappointed, as if he too wanted to come home.

"I love you, Beau."

"Love you too."

"Ellison?" My aunt was back on the line.

"Aunt Sis, how are they?"

"Fine. You don't need to worry. Listen, I got a call today. A friend of mine from Florida will be visiting Kansas City. She's a fan of your work and would love to meet you this weekend."

"Honoria Miller?"

"How did you know?"

"I've been invited to her grandson's engagement party."

"According to Honoria, her daughter-in-law is—"

"A nightmare?"

"The worst thing that ever happened to their family."

"I'm surprised. Marilyn says Price is a very nice young man. She did something right."

"Price isn't her son. Morton's first wife died, and he married Donna with embarrassing alacrity. At least according to Honoria. You'll adore her. Imagine a dragon with a sense of humor."

"I look forward to meeting her."

"Any progress on the case?"

I glanced at my husband, who was crouched on the kitchen floor, petting the dogs. I had so much to tell him. And none of it good.

"I found a body today. Chances are it's linked to Baxter's murder."

"Another mob hit?"

"That remains to be seen."

Anarchy looked up sharply.

"Aunt Sis, Anarchy and I haven't really spoken since I found the body. I should probably hang up."

"All right, dear. Call if you need anything."

"I will. Thank you. For everything."

"Ellison! Wait!"

"What is it?"

"Beau wants to talk to Anarchy."

"He's right here." I offered my husband the receiver.

Anarchy and Beau spent a few minutes chatting about baseball.

I was starting to think talking about sports was some sort of male secret language. Uncomfortable dinner party? Baseball. Difficulty expressing emotions? Baseball. Sadly, baseball wouldn't hide me from my litany of sins. Not when I could only name a few Royals players.

"When you get back, we'll go to a game. That's a promise." Anarchy hung up the phone.

"You may want a drink." I definitely did. I crossed to the fridge, grabbed a bottle of wine, and poured myself a generous glass.

"What's wrong?"

"I went to Club K this morning." The words came out in a rush.

Anarchy stared at me; his face unreadable.

"Baxter and Audrey met there on Thursday nights. He showed up last Thursday. She didn't."

"You knew her well?"

I shrugged. "Her husband had an affair with Madeline Harper before Henry did. Our kids attend the same school."

"So, Baxter Phelps was cheating on his wife."

A gulp of wine later, I continued. "Audrey had another friend —someone Kathleen wouldn't tell me about."

"What else?"

I felt like a tightrope walker without a net, one misstep away from falling and bringing my marriage crashing upon me.

"Frank followed me there."

"Frank?"

"The man in black."

"He followed you?" Anarchy's open palm passed over his eyes. "And you got his name?"

My throat was dry. "Just his first name."

He shook his head disbelief. "I asked you to be careful."

"I was." Sort of.

"You went to Audrey's because Kathleen Mahoney told you about Audrey's relationship with Baxter."

"Yes."

"What did Frank do?"

"He followed me."

Anarchy exhaled sharply.

"Did he go inside with you?"

"No."

"Thank, God," he muttered.

"You found the body, then what?"

"Frank left." No way was I admitting that I'd told him to leave.

"Anything else?"

"I went to see Helen Phelps today. She wasn't home, but her neighbor swears Helen didn't leave her house on Thursday night."

"So, she has an alibi."

"When I got home, Donna Miller was here. I'm pretty sure she went through the files on your desk."

Anarchy switched things up and ran his hand over the back of his neck.

"Then there's tonight."

"Tonight?"

"Before you arrived, Sandy Wilcox told me that Grant had dinner with Lloyd Crowder on Thursday."

"He lied to his wife. Either that or Elizabeth Crowder lied to you."

"She didn't. Grace and I had lunch at Nabil's when we went shopping. I asked the maître d'. He confirmed the Crowders were there for dinner last Thursday."

Anarchy leaned against the counter, tilting his head toward the ceiling. "I might have made a mistake with Baxter Phelps."

Might have? I bit my lips, I'd already said more than enough.

"I've been so focused on one outcome that I didn't consider other possibilities."

"Do you still think it's a member of the mafia?" My voice was soft, tentative, hopeful. Had I truly convinced him?

"At this point, I have no idea." He sighed. "You've had a busy day."

"You're not mad?"

He pulled me against his chest, and some of the tightness in my neck released. He wasn't mad. Married to Henry, I'd grown accustomed to a man who treated me like a mentally challenged child. If I'd disregarded one of Henry's edicts, he would have been furious. I'd forgotten that Anarchy looked upon me as an equal. He might not like my decisions, but he respected my right to make them.

"I'm not thrilled you went to Club K. I'm really not thrilled about Frank. But if I had listened to you, maybe that wouldn't have happened." He raked his fingers through his hair. "What do you know about Audrey's ex-husband?"

"Like I said, Gibson had an affair with Madeline. She

dumped him for Henry, and Audrey divorced him. Or maybe he divorced her. I can't remember. It was not a friendly divorce."

"I'll talk to him tomorrow. Can you think of any reason he'd kill Baxter or Audrey?"

"No. How did she die?"

"Shot to the chest."

"Same gun as the one that killed Baxter?"

"We're running ballistics."

"What about Grant Wilcox?"

Anarchy tilted his head. "What about him?"

I didn't like him, "He's full of theories and he lied to his wife about where he was on Thursday."

"Any other suspects?"

"Donna Miller."

"Why? Because she snooped?"

"Yes. Also, when I was at her house for the luncheon, she led with my art."

"What do you mean?"

"No one in Kansas City leads with my art. It's either 'Ellison finds bodies' or 'Ellison is married to a homicide detective.' Never my art. We're going to a party at the Millers' on Friday night. Maybe you can get a feel for her then."

He pulled me closer and tucked a strand of hair behind my ear. "You've had a rough day."

"Maybe."

"You worried about telling me all this, didn't you?"

I nodded.

"You never need to worry. I might not like some of the things you do, but I'll never stop loving you. Thank you for being honest with me."

"Thank you for understanding."

A smile curled his lips. "I think we should thank each other upstairs."

CHAPTER FOURTEEN

I sat in the card room at the club with Jinx and Libba. We were waiting for our perennially late fourth, Daisy.

Jinx made a show of glancing at her watch. "Where is she?"

I caught Libba's eye and raised my brows in a have-you-talked-to-Charlie glance.

She pursed her lips, shook her head, and side-eyed Jinx. Libba might adore our gossipy friend, but Charlie's proposal and her answer were private. "She's only five minutes late. That's nothing for Daisy."

"But she's not here," Jinx grumbled.

"Yes, I am." Daisy slid into her empty seat and offered an apologetic grin. "The babysitter had questions about the sched-ule." I'm sure the schedule was daunting. Daisy had many, many kids, and getting them to the right lessons, practices, and play dates at the right time was a full-time job. She drew a card from the deck fanned across the table and showed us the six of hearts.

Jinx won the draw with the queen of diamonds and began to deal. "So, Ellison, Audrey Miles."

"What about her?"

"A little bird told me your car was parked in front of her house before the police arrived."

"I was hoping to keep that quiet." Mother would not be pleased.

"So, you did find her?" Jinx looked up from dealing the cards.

"You found another body?" Daisy didn't even sound surprised.

"I'm afraid so."

"How did she die?" asked Jinx.

"You know I can't comment on Anarchy's cases."

"So, it was murder. Do you think Gibson killed her?"

"I don't see why. They were already divorced. Besides, Gibson took the kids on vacation. He wasn't even in town when Audrey died." Assuming she died on Thursday night.

"He had to pay her alimony. Generous alimony. And I heard she'd taken a...turn." Jinx dealt the last card.

"What does that mean?" Daisy picked up her hand and began to sort.

"She liked kinky sex," Jinx replied.

"No!" Daisy dropped the queen of clubs on the table, quickly returning the card to her hand.

How did Jinx know what Audrey got up to at Club K? "Who's your source?" I asked.

"Oh, please. Audrey Miles was a consenting adult. What she did in the bedroom is none of our business." Leave it to Libba to defend another woman's sex life. She shifted the cards in her hand and frowned.

Jinx snapped her cards closed. "Pass."

I had only nine points, ten if I counted a long club suit. "Pass."

"Pass," said Daisy.

"I hate this bid. Two clubs." Libba had twenty-two or more points.

"I'm out," said Jinx.

I reviewed my hand. No additional points had snuck in since my last bid. "Two no trump."

"Pass." Daisy offered up a sweet smile. "You two talk amongst yourselves."

Libba gazed at her cards for long seconds before saying, "Three hearts."

That meant she had at least four hearts. I had only two. One was the king, the other the three. "Three no trump."

"Six no trump."

"Libba!" She'd bid a small slam and left me to play it.

Daisy led the three of diamonds, and Libba laid down the dummy. Her hand was spectacular. I saw, at most, one loser.

"Back to the sex," said Jinx. "Does Anarchy think it got her killed?"

I took Daisy's three with the jack on the board. "I have no idea." Then, I led a low club to my hand and played the king. Daisy and Jinx both threw low cards. Next, I led a club back to the board.

Daisy threw the queen of clubs, and I couldn't help but smile. We were going to take every trick.

"Second hand low," Jinx scolded her.

"My only club," Daisy replied.

"I think the rest are yours."

I didn't disagree, but I played it out, taking every trick.

With a scowl, Jinx jotted down our score. "At least you weren't vulnerable." We'd scored five-hundred points instead of seven-hundred-fifty.

"Do you want to cut?" I nudged the deck toward her.

She cut thin. "You're sure you don't have anything to tell us about Audrey's death?"

I started to deal. "I don't. Have you heard anything?" The name of Audrey's second lover would be helpful. That or whoever told Jinx that Audrey indulged in kinky sex.

Jinx donned a mulish expression and shook her head. I'd get nothing out of her today.

I changed the subject. "What have we learned about Donna Miller?"

Jinx's brows lifted. "Why do you ask?"

"She seems an interesting woman." I kept my voice mild and focused on dealing the cards.

"What do you know?" she demanded.

"Not much. Aunt Sis is friends with her mother-in-law, Honoria. Donna is not Price's mother. She's Morton's second wife."

"Where's the first one?" asked Libba.

"She died."

"I wonder if the royal Danica was hers." Libba lifted her iced tea to her lips.

"I wonder if Donna killed her." We all gaped at sweet Daisy, and she flushed. "It's just that she seems…grasping. That might extend to another woman's husband."

Jinx chuckled. "You think Donna Miller killed Morton's first wife so she could marry him?"

"Stranger things have happened." And I'd seen many of them. "A grieving man. A pretty woman ready to comfort him."

"That we've all seen," Jinx conceded. "But murder?"

"A rich man makes a good motive."

"You really don't like her."

"I found her going through a file on Anarchy's desk."

"What was she doing in your house?"

"She showed up, demanding to see my studio. When Aggie told her I wasn't home, she refused to leave."

"What did she say when you caught her snooping?"

"She went on the offensive."

"Hmm." Jinx rubbed her chin. "Where are the Millers from?"

"Boston."

Her eyes gleamed with a sharp desire for fresh gossip. "I'll make a few calls and let you know. What can you tell me about Baxter's death?"

"Nothing you don't already know."

"Try me."

"Behner found Baxter's body after chasing away a group of pool-hopping kids. Baxter was shot."

"Is Anarchy still looking at a mob connection?"

"I don't think he's ruled out any avenue. Are you going to the funeral?" It was planned for tomorrow afternoon.

"I am. You?"

"Yes."

"And Anarchy?"

He might not sit with me, but he'd be there. He said a surprising number of killers attended their victims' funerals. "He'll attend. Has anyone talked to Helen recently?"

"I heard she was staying with Chipper," said Jinx. Exactly what I'd heard.

"Are we going to play bridge?" Libba groused.

"Sorry." I picked up my cards, quickly sorting. "One heart."

"Pass," said Daisy.

"Four hearts," Libba replied with a smirk at Jinx.

"Not our day, Daisy. Pass."

We played cards until Daisy glanced at her watch and gasped. "Oh, Lord, is that time? I must fly. The sitter is going to kill me." If the sitter was smart, she'd have accounted for Daisy's usual tardiness. She grabbed her handbag and hurried out the door.

"Of course," said Jinx. "The first decent hand I've had in an hour."

The cards were like that. One day you couldn't win. The next day you couldn't lose.

I SAT IN THE BACK OF THE CHURCH AND WATCHED THE PEWS IN front of me fill. Well-heeled, well-tanned women in navy or black dresses. Similar colors for the men, but instead of black suits, they wore gray.

The sanctuary's ribbed ceiling arched above me.

"Such a pretty church." Liz Brandt slid in next to me.

"Uncomfortable pews." I shifted, trying to ignore the dull ache in my back.

"There is that." Liz smoothed black linen over her lap. "New dress?"

"I picked it up at Swanson's when I took Grace back-to-school shopping." The navy dress was somehow both chic and demure.

"I haven't been in weeks. I need to see what Esme has in for fall."

The woman sitting in front of us twisted in her seat and scowled, clearly unimpressed with our talk of shopping at a funeral.

I offered her an apologetic smile and fell silent.

"Are you going to the reception?" asked Liz.

Helen had opted for punch and cookies in the church basement.

"Just to pay my respects."

The judgmental woman snorted.

"Is Perry coming?"

"He had a hearing he couldn't reschedule."

"That's too bad. We had a lovely time at your party."

"We're so glad you could come. Is Anarchy here?"

The woman in front of us turned again. "A little respect?"

"Sorry," I apologized.

Next to me, Liz rolled her eyes and opened her mouth as if she had a smart reply at the ready, but the organ interrupted her.

The woman turned toward the front of the church, and Liz

and I fell silent as Helen, her daughter, and Chipper and his family filed into the front pews.

The service was simple, the homily generic, the hymns expected. Mother, who rated funerals on a ten-point scale, would have given it a six.

Since the church emptied from front to back, Liz and I stood at the end of the line to pay our respects.

"Look," she said. "There's Kate Barron." Kate attended funerals. Her parents' friends. Her friends. Acquaintances. Her husband's business associates. She attended them all. It was either terribly sweet or terribly eccentric. Since I liked Kate, I was going with sweet.

"She must have a whole closet of black and navy." Along with sensible pumps and matching handbags. "I think it would be terribly depressing. Celebrations of life seldom seem celebratory."

We inched forward and Liz frowned. "What is she doing here?"

"Who?"

"Donna Miller."

"Where?"

"There." She pointed discreetly at a woman in a black Chanel suit. "Does she even know Helen?"

"No idea. Are you going to the engagement party?"

"Perry and I didn't make the cut." She did not sound remotely upset at being left off the guest list. "I hear it's a small affair. You're going?"

"We are."

"You'll have to tell me what Donna wears. I'm not sure what I think of her personally, but the woman has style." She frowned. "What are you wearing?"

"Do you remember that Bill Blass I brought home from Chicago?" The dress had a boho vibe. Loose chiffon covered a black satin slip, and black sequins had been hand sewn onto the delicate fabric. It was light and airy and absolutely perfect for a summer cocktail party.

Liz nodded. Her seal of approval wasn't lightly given, if she thought the dress was perfect, it was.

The line lurched forward a few feet. "I heard Gibson is planning Audrey's funeral. I think it will be next Tuesday." She shook her blonde head. "Poor woman."

"Yes." No one deserved to die like that. No one deserved to lie in a congealed pool of their own blood, unfound, for days.

"Such a blessing that Gibson had taken the kids on vacation." She wrinkled her nose and shuddered. "I heard the body…"

No matter what she imagined, what I'd seen (and smelled) when I found Audrey was worse. "Anarchy's investigating her murder."

"Really? Hers and Baxter's?"

I wasn't about to mention that the two deaths were probably related. "Where did Gibson take the kids?"

"Colorado. Gibson's sister has a place in Breck. They were supposed to leave last Thursday, but something came up, and Gibson delayed a day. They left before dawn on Friday morning." She shook her head. "What a drive. No one to spell you and two children in the back seat. The children are still in Colorado. Gibson left them with his sister and flew back to Kansas City."

So, Gibson Miles had been in town on Thursday night. But what reason did he have to kill Audrey? If he'd learned about her new lifestyle? I would have done almost anything to protect Grace from learning about Henry's proclivities. But murder?

People had killed for lesser reasons.

I wondered if Anarchy had interviewed him yet.

"Ellison?"

"I'm sorry, what?"

"You were a million miles away." Liz gave my arm a gentle tug, and we closed the difference between us and the next person in line.

"Did you know her well?"

"Audrey? No."

"So, you'll skip the funeral?"

"I don't know." The gossip at funerals and weddings was second to none. Perhaps that was why Kate Barron attended so many.

"If you decide to go, let me know. We can drive together. It's at St. Andrew's, and you know what the parking is like. The last time I attended a funeral there, I had to park halfway to Ward Parkway."

"Will do. Let's talk about something other than funerals and death."

"Have you been to any Royals games lately?"

"No."

"You need to go. The third baseman is absolutely darling."

Here I was, at a funeral, actually talking baseball. Sort of.

CHAPTER FIFTEEN

Anarchy, looking incredibly handsome in his charcoal-gray suit, crisp white shirt and Hermès tie, tucked my arm into his elbow as the valet drove off with our car. His face was tense, as if we were heading into battle rather than a party.

"We don't have to stay long," I murmured.

He looked down at me, the crinkles at the corners of his eyes betraying his amusement. "There will be cocktails."

"Yes," I allowed.

"They'll try to serve dinner at seven-thirty, but it'll be eight before everyone is seated." He wasn't wrong. "And we can't eat and run. There's no way we're here for anything less than three hours."

"I'll make it up to you."

Interest flared in his brown eyes. "Oh?"

Rising onto my tiptoes, I kissed the corner of his mouth. "I promise."

"You drive a hard bargain, Mrs. Jones."

"I hope so."

Anarchy was laughing as the front door swung open,

revealing Donna and the man I assumed was her husband. Morton Miller had one of those thin New England faces that grew craggy with age. He was distinguished, the perfect foil for his wife's polished blonde perfection.

Donna offered me a chilly smile. "Ellison, how nice to see you again and what a...pretty dress."

I pretended not to hear the insult but responded in kind, "I love your suit. Not everyone can wear that color."

Donna's smile went from chilly to arctic, and her husband hurried to close the gap between us. He extended a hand toward Anarchy. "Morton Miller. So glad you could join us this evening."

"Anarchy Jones."

The two men shook.

"Anarchy is a unique name." Donna didn't mean unique, she meant weird.

My husband shifted his gaze to our hostess and extended his hand. "I'm originally from the San Francisco area. My parents were hippies long before the sixties."

"Where in San Francisco?" asked Morton.

"Palo Alto."

Morton nodded as if he approved. "I have several friends who went to Stanford."

"My alma mater," Anarchy replied.

"Really?" The surprise in Donna's voice was insulting. "You went to Stanford and became a homicide detective?"

"I hate being chained to a desk, and justice is important to me," he replied smoothly.

Donna flushed, even as her lips thinned to a narrow line. "There's a bar set up in the living room. Ellison, you remember the way?"

We'd been dismissed.

"I do. Thank you."

We stepped away from our hosts, but I still heard Morton

whisper, "What the hell was that? Those people are guests in our home!"

I didn't hear her reply.

Emma Tremblay stood just inside the living room entrance with a young man who could only be Morton's son. She offered us a sweet smile. "Mr. and Mrs. Jones, we're so pleased you could celebrate with us."

"We're delighted to be included." I couldn't help but glance at Emma's left hand. Her bare left hand.

Price, who was shaking hands with Anarchy, must have noticed because he said, "It's a family tradition. After dinner, I'll get down on one knee and officially ask Emma to be my wife."

"And I'll say yes," Emma added, looking at Price with stars in her eyes.

"I believe my grandmother wants to meet Mrs. Jones," he said, offering me his arm.

"Anything from the bar?" asked Anarchy.

"Gin and tonic, please."

He nodded. "I'll find you."

Honoria Miller sat ramrod straight in a wingback chair near the hearth. Like her son and grandson, Mrs. Miller had a thin face. Her snowy-white hair was pulled into a tight bun, and her sharp eyes gleamed with intelligence.

"Gram, this is Ellison Jones. Mrs. Jones, this is my gram, Honoria Miller." He retreated a step, looking over his shoulder at Emma.

"Go," his grandmother told him. "Spend your evening with Emma."

He left us, and I produced a polite smile. "It's a pleasure to meet you, Mrs. Miller. I believe you know my aunt."

"Indeed, I do." She motioned to the empty wingback chair angled near hers.

I sat, crossing my ankles and folding my hands in my lap. "Aunt Sis sends her regards."

"Your aunt is one of my favorite people. I don't think I've ever met anyone who's more fun." She studied me. "Are you fun?"

"Honestly, no."

She barked a short laugh. "And Sis can't paint. The good Lord spreads out his gifts."

"How are you finding Kansas City?"

"I arrived this afternoon. Emma and Price took me to the Country Club Plaza."

"Some of our best stores and restaurants."

"Everyone was so friendly," she complained. "They acted as if we'd known each other for years."

"We're Midwesterners. We can't help it." On the east coast, population density and ridiculous commutes made people cranky. Also, the evening news came on at eleven. Who could stay up late night after night, then get up for work and be pleasant?

She shook her head as if Midwestern friendliness was an intractable problem. "Price seems to like it here. Then again, he met a lovely girl. How long have you known her family?"

I didn't miss the sharp glint in her eyes. "Forever. In fact, I believe Aunt Sis may have dated Marilyn Tremblay's father when they were in high school."

Honoria Miller's perfect posture relaxed the tiniest bit. "She never said."

"My aunt went to college and never looked back. I doubt she knows who John Willoughby's daughter married."

"Willoughby?" Philadelphia had its Main Line. Virginia had its first families. And Boston had its Brahmins. Willoughby was a Brahmin name. "Is he here, tonight?"

"I imagine so." And I had no doubt Honoria would quiz John about his family tree.

"What do you think of my daughter-in-law?"

Her blunt question surprised me, and I shifted in my seat

searching for a diplomatic answer. "She's done a beautiful job with this house."

"She hires good decorators."

"She dresses well."

A slow smile spread across Honoria's face. "You don't care for her."

"You can't expect me to insult my hostess."

She wrinkled her nose. "Someone raised you well. Although Sis says you find bodies."

"Not on purpose," I said dryly.

She barked a laugh as Anarchy put a drink in my hand.

I flashed him a look of pure gratitude. "Anarchy, this is Mrs. Miller, Price's grandmother. Mrs. Miller, my husband, Anarchy Jones."

"A pleasure to make your acquaintance, ma'am."

Mrs. Miller gave him a long look. "Likewise. You're the homicide detective?"

"Yes, ma'am."

"You two make quite a pair."

"We try, ma'am."

Her eyes twinkled. "Stop calling me ma'am. You make me feel older than the hills."

"As you wish, Mrs. Miller."

"You have nice manners, young man. I should let you mingle, especially since you're at my table for dinner and the fireworks."

Idly, I wondered how they'd managed to get a fireworks permit in Mission Hills.

"Ellison?"

"Yes, Mrs. Miller?"

"Call me Honoria and tell Price I'd like to meet John Willoughby." Her voice brooked no argument. Aunt Sis was right. Honoria was a dragon. And I liked her.

"As you wish."

Dinner was served in the conservatory—four tables of eight, five courses, each course perfectly paired with a different wine. It was approaching ten o'clock before Price led Emma to the center of the room.

"Here come the fireworks," Honoria murmured.

Price sank to one knee and reached into his pocket. "Emma, I love you and always will. Will you do me the honor of becoming my wife?"

He opened the ring box and slipped a ring onto her finger.

"I love you, too. Of cou—"

"That's mine!" Donna's cheeks were flushed, and she pointed at Emma's finger with single-minded focus. "Mine! Give it to me!"

Price didn't move, but Emma turned to the woman shrieking at her. The girl looked confused, as if Donna's demand wasn't perfectly clear.

"Give. It. To. Me." Donna launched herself at her future daughter-in-law, tackling her to the floor.

Fortunately, someone had laid a thick rug in the conservatory's center, likely to protect Price's knees. But the deep pile saved Emma's head from the tiles.

If Donna felt the impact, she ignored it. She was too busy trying to claw the ring off of Emma's hand.

"Donna!" Morton sounded horrified. Mortified. Appalled. But he didn't move to disentangle his wife from his son's future wife.

I glanced at Honoria. She was grinning from ear to ear. Almost as if she'd planned this.

Anarchy stood, and I quickly grabbed his wrist, keeping him at the table. We did not want to wade into this mess.

"Donna, stop this." Morton was loud enough to get his wife's attention.

She turned her vicious expression on her husband. "It's mine! You said I could have it!"

Price found some initiative and attempted to pull his step-mother off of Emma. Donna fought back, swinging wildly, striking him on the chin.

His head snapped backward, and he collapsed in a heap.

"Kid has got a glass jaw," Anarchy muttered.

Meanwhile, Emma fought back, landing a blow on Donna's nose. The resulting crunching sound made me cringe.

"The girl's got a good left hook."

I gaped at my husband before shifting my gaze to Honoria. "These are your fireworks?" This wasn't fireworks. This was a brawl. If Emma agreed marry Price after this disaster, the night would follow them the rests of their lives.

She nodded, clearly pleased with herself. "It's about time Morton sees that awful woman for what she is." She stood. "It's my ring. I gave it to Price." Honoria's voice was clear as a bell. And loud. "It was never yours and never will be."

Honoria's announcement distracted Donna, and Morton was able to grab her, dragging her away from his unconscious son, Emma, and the ring.

"Bitch!" Donna shrieked. She struggled against her husband's hold, and I worried for Honoria's safety if she got free.

"Gold-digging hussy." There was no real heat behind Honoria's words. It was as if she was stating self-evident facts.

I silently prayed the floor would open and swallow Anarchy and me whole.

Donna struggled against her husband's grip. Uselessly. He hauled her into the front hall.

Honoria resumed her seat. "I've never liked that woman. Or trusted her. Or believed a single word out of her mouth. She claims to be from Ohio, but I can hear the Jersey shore in her voice. If she's who she says she is, I'll eat my best hat."

"What do you mean?" I asked.

"Donna Barksdale. Pfft. She claims she attended Miami of

Ohio. Graduated with a marketing degree. Came to Boston to work for an ad agency."

Anarchy showed sudden interest. "What year did she graduate?"

"She says she graduated in 1952. There was a Donna Barksdale who attended Miami of Ohio. The poor girl's parents died in an accident her senior year. I don't know what happened to her, but that woman—" Honoria jerked her head toward where Donna had disappeared "—took her place."

Was Honoria as crazy as Donna?

"I've told my son over and over again, but he's too blind to see. Tonight proved my point."

All it proved that Donna was crazy.

"What about Emma?" The poor girl, who'd pulled Price onto her lap, was sobbing.

As I watched, his eyes fluttered open.

"Emma will be fine," Honoria assured me. "The girl has Willoughby blood. That means she's got gumption. And being the new owner of a four-carat diamond ring doesn't hurt either.

"I'M WALKING WITH JINX THIS MORNING," I STARED AT ANARCHY over the rim of my coffee cup.

"Where?" He was dressed for work in khaki pants and a plaid jacket, one the cleaners hadn't lost yet. I'd remedy that soon.

"Not my usual route. I thought I'd put the dogs in the car and go to her house. We can walk in her neighborhood. They need it desperately—if they don't burn off some energy, Aggie may kill them." Another lasagna episode might push her over the edge.

"Promise me you'll stay vigilant."

"Promise." I wanted to ask about the case but was trying to

keep my distance after how over involved I'd been earlier in the week.

"Go ahead and ask," Anarchy said. The man could read me like a book.

"Any suspects?"

"We're bringing in Kathleen Mahoney. Maybe she'll be more forthcoming sitting in a police interrogation room."

I took a sip of coffee. "You want her to tell you about Audrey's other lover?"

"Exactly."

"Who else?"

"Donna Miller."

"Donna?"

"The woman is crazy," Anarchy said flatly.

"Why would she kill Baxter?"

"He graduated from Miami University in 1952. Maybe he knew the real Donna."

"But why kill Audrey?"

"Collateral damage."

"Who else?"

"That's it."

"Not Gibson?"

"He was in Colorado."

"Not according to Liz," I countered. "She says he left early Friday morning."

"How does she know?"

"They live across the street from each other. I imagine she saw him leave." I glanced at the clock and winced. Jinx wanted to walk before it got too hot, and I'd promised to be at her house by eight. "I should get going." With considerable effort, I clipped leashes onto the dancing dogs' collars.

"Be careful." Anarchy's words followed me out the back door, and I smiled softly, hearing the real concern behind them. Then, I loaded the dogs into the car.

Less than five minutes later, I parked in front of Jinx's house. Apparently, she'd been waiting, because she immediately emerged with her cocker spaniel, Groucho.

Naming a dog after a comedian was asking for trouble, and Groucho didn't disappoint. He hid slippers, chewed purse straps, made runs for freedom, and created mayhem. Jinx adored him.

Groucho wagged his tail so fast his whole body shook. Then, he tugged on his leash until Jinx joined us at the curb. The dogs sniffed each other.

"I'm so grateful that humans shake hands." Jinx pulled Groucho's nose away from Max's hiney.

"Where to?" I asked.

"I usually cut over to Fairway."

"Lead the way."

We'd walked only a few steps when she said, "I heard last night's party was memorable."

"Finn, leave it." I yanked him away from a wadded paper napkin in the gutter. "Very memorable. Especially for poor Emma."

"Is she still going to marry him?"

"If you saw the ring, you wouldn't even ask that question."

We turned right on Overhill Road.

"Did Donna really tackle her?"

"Yes. Finn, no." The Airedale was watching a squirrel with intent, and I didn't want my arm ripped from its socket.

"What did Marilyn say?" Jinx asked.

"She was horrified. Donna will be Emma's mother-in-law. Who's to say the carving knife doesn't slip at Thanksgiving? Emma might lose a finger."

"She's that crazy?"

I felt Jinx's gaze as I nodded. "I've never seen anything like it."

"So, the husband dragged her off, then what happened?"

"Honoria told the staff to serve Champagne—"

"I heard it was Veuve."

"You heard right. When she had a glass in hand, she toasted Price and his new fiancée, of whom she wholeheartedly approves."

"She said that?" Jinx sounded mildly impressed.

"She did." I tightened my grip on Max's leash. We were between two golf courses, and if he escaped, he'd disrupt golf games left and right.

We crossed Indian Creek, leaving Mission Hills and entering Fairway, then turned left, limiting the number of golf courses Max could disrupt to one. I breathed a little easier, but I still kept a death grip on his leash.

We passed Norwood Street, and Jinx slowed her steps. "Any news about Audrey?"

Audrey's house was on Norwood. "How did you know she was visiting a sex club?"

She shook her head.

I thought for a moment, then answered my own question. "The person who told you goes there, too."

"Bingo."

That was disturbing. Just how many people of my acquaintance went to Club K? "Was it Prudence?"

"Heavens, no." She sounded offended I'd suggested such a thing.

"Who?" I insisted.

Finn took advantage of my inattention, jerking free of my hold on his leash. With a happy bark, he raced down Fairway Road.

"Finn! Here—" I forced Max's leash into Jinx's free hand. "Hold on to Max." Then, I ran after my dog.

He glanced over his shoulder, grinned, and ran faster. Chase was one of his favorite games.

"Finn!"

Happiness trailed behind him like a kite's tail.

"Finn!"

He took a sharp right, dashing into someone's backyard.

Dammit! "Finn!" I tried to keep the annoyance out of my voice. No dog comes for an angry owner. "Finn, I have treats." It was a lie. "Please, buddy, come get a treat."

I wiped the sweat off my forehead and barged into a stranger's backyard.

Finn wasn't there.

Woof!

I recognized his bark. It was nearby. "Finn!"

Saying a silent apology to the homeowner, I ventured further into their backyard. There was no fence, and Finn had switched his game to the next block.

"Finn!"

The house's backdoor opened.

"I'm so very sorry. For disturbing you. For trespassing. For—"

"Here." The homeowner held out a dog biscuit. "Happens around here all the time. Go ahead and cut through. The Clarks won't mind."

"Thank you." I accepted the biscuit and cut back to Norwood.

Finn was in a yard two doors down—thankfully a front yard.

"I've got a biscuit for you, buddy."

His stubby tail wagged.

"Come get it." I approached slowly.

He danced a few steps backward and whined softly. Biscuit or chase? That was the conundrum.

"It's a yummy treat," I wheedled.

He inched forward, and I grabbed his leash. When I had him firmly in hand, I let him chomp on the biscuit.

"You are a very bad dog."

His tail wagged. He didn't care.

I was halfway to the street before I noticed the yellow crime tape at the front door. Finn had led me to Audrey's house.

"Ugh. Only you would lead me to a crime scene." Not strictly true. Given half a chance, Max would do the same. "Come on." I headed us toward the corner.

We were almost there when I felt the weight of someone's gaze on the back of my neck.

With a sigh, I turned and said, "Hello, Frank."

CHAPTER SIXTEEN

S weat didn't trickle down my back. No, it ran in steady rivulets. And when my tongue touched my lips, I tasted salt. But, I'd done it. Jinx and I had walked for miles, and the dogs were worn out. My hand closed around the door and I paused, letting the anticipation build. The feeling of being ready to melt, then walking into a well air-conditioned house was delicious—one of summer's true pleasures. How Sherry Patterson lived without it was a mystery.

The dogs agreed with me about air-conditioning. They dashed inside, drained their water bowl, then flopped onto the cool floor, their tongues lolling out of their smiling mouths.

I refilled their bowl, poured myself a glass of iced tea, and read the note Aggie had left for me on the counter.

There's a Bundt in the pantry, chicken salad in the fridge, and plenty of fixings for sandwiches. Call if you need me. Aggie.

There was no way I'd interrupt Aggie's Saturday with her boyfriend.

Making sure the pantry door was firmly closed (the dogs weren't above eating a Bundt), I headed upstairs for a shower.

It wasn't until I stood under a steady stream of tepid water that I allowed myself to think about my conversation with Frank. I'd told him Anarchy was pursuing other suspects, and he'd nodded his approval. "Make sure he does."

I didn't think Frank would hurt me. I was fairly certain he found me amusing. Still, there was something terrifying about him. Carefully contained violence coupled with a complete lack of empathy. I didn't make the mistake of thinking Frank was safe. He wasn't. And I was glad that the kids remained in Colorado.

A pang in my chest reminded me just how empty the house was without them.

I needed to call them, and take the Bundt to Gibson Miles, and check in on Libba.

With a plan for the rest of my day, I turned off the water and wrapped myself in a fluffy towel.

Brnng, brnng.

I secured the towel and hurried into the bedroom.

Brnng, brnng.

"Hello."

"Ellison." My father's voice carried down the line.

My heart stuttered. My father only ever phoned me for a round of golf. Since he was in Michigan and I was in Missouri, I was fairly certain that wasn't the reason for his call. "Daddy? Are you okay? Has something happened to Mother?"

"Did you find a body?" He sounded angry.

I imagined him in his study at the house on Harbor Point—the pine floors, the comfortable furniture, the bowls of glassies scavenged on the beach. He had a spectacular view of the lake. The kind of peaceful view that made ire difficult to maintain. "I did. In my defense, it's not my fault."

"Did you send Grace and Beau to your aunt in Colorado?"

"I did." And I'd hoped my parents never found out.

"You sent them to Sis, not us. Your mother is beside herself."

"We needed to get them someplace safe on very short notice.

As we were putting them on a flight to Denver, Aunt Sis was leaving Vail to be at the airport when they landed. You and Mother couldn't have done that. Both Detroit and Chicago are too far away from Harbor Point."

He grunted, unable to argue with my logic. "This is because Anarchy's investigating the mob?"

"Anarchy is investigating a murder. A mob hit is just one possibility." I heard whispered words in the background. Mother was with him.

"What prompted this sudden decision to whisk the children to safety? You assured your mother everyone was fine, that there was nothing to worry about."

"Things changed." It was a weak response but telling Daddy that someone from the mafia had followed Grace to one of her friend's houses was a no go.

Again, I heard whispers. Angry whispers.

"You could have flown to Michigan with the children and stayed here. If they're in danger, you are, too."

I perched on the edge of the bed, gathered my courage, and said, "Just put her on the phone."

"I don't think that's a good idea." In other words, Mother was having a faunching fit. She was worried and angry and hurt, and Daddy was concerned that she'd say something unforgivable.

"Daddy, I'm doing the best I can. So is Anarchy. As soon as he's caught the killer, we'll bring the kids home."

"Are you involved in his investigation?"

"Other than passing on what gossip I hear, no." I chose not to dwell on the Bundt cake waiting in the pantry.

"Keep it that way. We worry about you."

"I know. And I'm sorry."

"Just think how you'd feel if Grace got herself involved in a murder investigation." If she was an adult, I liked to think that I'd give her more credit than my parents gave me.

"I get it, Daddy. I do. And I appreciate that you care. Thank you for calling."

"We love you, punkin." The endearment sounded almost grudging. "Stay safe." He hung up.

I groaned. Loudly. Then I let my head drop. Mother and Daddy were coming home the Tuesday after Labor Day. Not nearly enough time for Mother, who could nurse a grudge like nobody's business, to cool off. I gave myself a moment to feel the dread coursing through my veins, then I straightened my shoulders and stood. Mother and her ire were a problem for another day.

Brnng, brnng.

I looked at the phone like it was a coiled snake (and I *hated* snakes).

Brnng, brnng.

With a sense of impending doom hanging over my head like a dark storm cloud, I picked up the receiver. "Jones residence."

"Tell me everything," Aunt Sis demanded. "Did she really tackle Price's fiancée?"

I recounted everything I could remember about the party, my conversation with Honoria, and the terrible scene with Donna.

"Honoria has never trusted her. She felt the circumstances of Morton's first wife's death were odd, then Donna was just there."

Had Daisy been right in her suspicions? "Odd how?"

"It was a one car accident. Poor Anne's car flipped, and her neck was broken."

"Honoria seems to think that Donna has stolen another woman's identity."

"Stranger things have happened. Honoria is extending her stay in Kansas City. If you and Anarchy give the all-clear for the kids to come home, I'll fly back with them so that I can see her."

"Are they around? Can I talk to them?"

"We hired a guide to take them river rafting. They'll be back later this afternoon."

I swallowed a disappointed sigh. "I'll call later."

"Take care of yourself, Ellison. And that handsome husband, too."

"I will. Thanks for everything, Aunt Sis."

"My pleasure, dear."

We hung up, and I got dressed, praying the phone didn't ring again.

It didn't. And thirty minutes later, I was in my car with Aggie's Bundt cake sitting next to me in the passenger seat. The enticing scents of cinnamon and pecan escaped from the covered lid, and I briefly considered keeping the cake. No. I did not need the calories hanging around. And without Beau, who could polish off half a cake in two days, the Bundt would be a constant temptation.

I parked in front of Gibson's house and counted cars. The poor man was inundated. Audrey's untimely death was an opportunity for divorcées to draw his attention. I was no competition to them, and I had cake. With a fair amount of confidence, I marched up the front walk and rang the bell.

Liz answered the door, smiling when she saw what I carried. "Is that what I think it is?"

"One of Aggie's Bundts? Yes."

"Come in, come in." She ushered me inside. "Poor Gibson is in the living room. I bet he'll be thrilled to see you." Liz took the cake from my hands and shooed me toward the grieving ex-husband.

Gibson stood when he saw me. "Ellison." He sounded like a drowning man who'd unexpectedly been thrown a life-preserver.

"Hey, Gib. I brought a cake."

"Thank you." He glanced at the bevy of divorcées cluttering up his living room, then said, "Do you have a few minutes to chat? I want your advice on the kids."

"Of course."

Eyes narrowed. Lips thinned. Was that a hiss?

Gib strode toward me. "We can talk in my study."

I turned and followed him, all too aware of the unhappy scowls burning holes through my linen shift.

He opened a door across the hall, ushering me into a paneled room with plaid carpet on the floor. Oxblood leather chairs sat in front of a large desk, hunting prints hung on the walls, and drapes that matched the carpet framed the windows. The room smelled of leather and cigars.

Gib sank into the chair behind the desk and dropped his head into his hands. He didn't look like a killer, he looked like a man adrift. But I'd been fooled before.

I sat across from him. "How can I help?"

"When Henry died, did you send Grace to a therapist?"

"I thought about it."

He nodded. "I don't know what to do."

Gibson's children were younger than Grace. "A therapist can't hurt. There are some who specialize in grief."

"Really? There are people who make grief their life's work?"

He winced and raked a hand through his thinning hair. "I...I don't know how to talk to them about their mother's death. They already think I'm the bad guy. They blame me for the divorce." The poor man looked as if he hadn't slept in days. "What am I going to do? Children need a mother."

There were five women in the living room who'd be happy to take the job. "Buck up. They still have a father who obviously loves them. Be there for them."

"But what do I tell them?" Most people had a hard time talking about death. Talking about murder was even harder. "Tell them their mother is in heaven and that the police are going to catch whoever hurt her."

"What else?"

"I didn't mourn Henry." There was no point in pretending I had. "But for Grace's sake, I've never spoken ill of him in her presence. Do that."

He stared at me with red-rimmed eyes, and his chest seemed to deflate. "You know about the club."

"I do."

"Who else knows?"

I shrugged. "Sometimes it seems as if half the people we know go there."

His shoulders slumped. "How could she?"

"I often wonder that about Henry's infidelities. Second guessing the dead gets you nowhere. Make sure the kids know their mother loved them. Allow them to grieve. Hire a therapist." *And, please, please, don't be the killer.* His children needed at least one parent.

"Thank you. I needed to hear that." He glanced at the door. "Do I have to go back out there?"

"Your harem awaits."

"Not funny, Ellison."

My lips quirked. "It's a little funny."

"I think I'm going to hide for a few minutes."

I stood. "Can't say as I blame you. Let me know if you or the kids need anything." I stepped into the hallway and nearly knocked Helen Phelps to the floor. Somehow, I managed to grab her elbow before she sank to the carpet. "Oh, my gracious! Helen! I'm so sorry. Are you alright?"

The woman looked gaunt; her eyes haunted. Whatever Baxter's faults (and they'd been many), it was clear that Helen mourned her husband. "I'm fine. I'm fine." She shook off my hand.

"How are you?" It was a stupid question. She was obviously struggling. Her hair needed a good wash and her dress was wrinkled.

She glared at me. "I talked to your husband yesterday. He asked me all sorts of questions about Baxter and some horrible club."

"He's trying to find Baxter's killer."

"The mob killed Baxter."

"Why?"

"I don't know." Her voice rose. "But he was shot in the head and left in the trunk of a car. That's a mob hit."

"They don't have exclusive rights."

"This isn't a joke, Ellison."

"I'm well aware."

"Your husband seems to think Baxter had some sort of fling with Audrey Miles. I don't believe it. He would never do that."

Husbands cheated. Baxter had definitely cheated. It didn't matter if Helen believed it or not. "I know how painful this is."

"Painful? Ha! Painful is being shot in the head. This is agony." She glared at me with additional venom. "Besides, what would you know about how I feel?"

How quickly people forgot. "My late husband cheated on me with multiple women, then he was murdered."

Her expression softened. Slightly. "Maybe you do know."

"You'd like to bring him back to life so you can kill him yourself?"

"How could he do this to me?"

"Exactly. After Henry was gone, there were nights when I lay in bed and thought about all the ways I wanted to kill him."

She gave a short, bitter laugh. "When did it get better?"

"It was a process. You're a strong woman; you'll make it through this." Helen was a rigid woman who'd had her life twisted completely out of shape. I had no idea if she was strong, but it seemed like the thing to say.

"Thank you, Ellison. I need to return your cake plate."

"Keep it. I buy them in bulk at K-Mart." The last thing someone who was grieving needed to do was worry about returning serving platters.

"You're sure?" She glanced down the hallway and shuddered.

"Positive. What's wrong?"

"Sandy Wilcox is here. She's appointed herself my keeper."

I winced on her behalf. "The kitchen is that way. Go." I pointed toward the back of the house. "I'll stall her for a while."

"Thank you." She scurried down the hall.

I turned and spotted Sandy. She stood in the entrance to the living room, clearly looking for Gib.

I approached slowly. I'd made Helen a promise, that didn't mean I was excited about keeping it. "Hello, Sandy."

She turned and offered me a bright smile. "I've been meaning to call you."

"Oh?"

She nodded with extreme vigor. "When we were at dinner, I told you that Grant met Lloyd Crowder for dinner the night Baxter was found. I made a mistake. He met with a business associate named Lloyd Cowherd. You can see how I confused the two."

All I could see was that Grant had offered his wife a cover story that wouldn't hold up. Incredibly, he'd come up with a worse one to replace it.

"Such a silly mistake," she continued. "I mean, I mentioned about Grant and Lloyd having dinner the other day when I was playing bridge, and Elizabeth Crowder told me it wasn't possible. She had dinner with her husband that night, after he'd met poor Baxter for a drink. Well, I went home and told Grant, and he cleared everything up. I misheard the name. That's all." She bit her lower lip and wrung her hands, as if she was desperate for me to believe her.

"Don't give it another thought."

"It's just that it looked bad for Grant, almost like he'd lied to me, when really I just misunderstood."

Was she so determined to keep her husband that she'd decided on blindness? I glanced into the living room filled with semi-desperate divorcées and withheld judgment. "Truly, I didn't think anything of it."

"Grant insisted that I clear things up."

I'd never liked Grant. The man was a poser. Worse, he treated the staff at the club poorly. Mother always said you could take a person's measure by how they treated the people who served them. Mother and I disagreed on many things, but she was right about that.

They way Sandy was tripping over herself making excuses for her husband, made me grit my teeth with annoyance.

None of this was her fault.

If anyone should be apologizing, it was Grant.

"There's nothing to clear up. Mistakes happen."

Her face cleared, and she glanced at the harpies (unkind, but true) in the living room. "I don't suppose you brought cake?"

I offered her a smile. "It's your lucky day."

CHAPTER SEVENTEEN

W hen I got home, I found Libba sitting at my
kitchen island drinking a martini. A pitcher sat
next to her elbow.

"Everything okay?" I dropped my purse on the counter, gave
the dogs a quick pet, and fetched myself a glass.

Her brows lifted. "You're drinking a martini?"

"It's been a long day." Such an understatement. "The real
question is why you're in my kitchen drinking gin by yourself.
Did something happen with Charlie?" The sharp bite of ice-cold
gin rolled across my tongue and down my thoat. If Libba had
added vermouth, the amount was undetectable.

She shifted her gaze to the oven, studying the reflection in its
glass with single-minded focus. "I told him what you told me to
say…"

Oh, dear Lord. I sank onto a stool and prepared for the worst.
Whatever had happened was going to be my fault. I braced
myself for tears or anger or—

"He said you were—I was—right. If we're going to get
married, we need to be each other's center."

"And what did you say?" I glanced at her hand. No ring.

"I told him if he could get his kids' approval, I'd marry him."
She took a sip. A large one. Her glass was half-empty when she
lowered the rim.

"That's happy news."

"It is," she agreed sadly.

"So, why are you drinking alone?" In my kitchen.

"They'll never give their approval."

If she really thought Charlie's kids would say "no," why had
she made her marriage contingent on their approval. I reached
out and squeezed her hand. "You don't know that."

"I do. They were monsters earlier this summer. As soon as
they figured out Charlie and I were serious, they hated me."

"Their mother was whispering poison in their ears."

"It's not like she'll ever stop."

"She will. She'll meet someone and put her energy into
loving him instead of hating Charlie."

"I just worry that this is all too soon." Aha! Now we were
getting somewhere. The kids weren't the real problem. They
were a stand-on for Libba's fears.

"You've waited decades for the exact right man, and it isn't
soon at all."

"Okay, Pollyana."

"I really don't feel like Pollyana, today." I took a large slug
of delicious gin.

Libba rooted around in the handbag that hung over the back
of her stool. "I want to hear all about it, but first, can I
smoke?"

"Outside."

She pouted. "It's hot outside."

"This time of day, the patio is in the shade. Also, we're not
done talking about you."

"Will you come outside with me? Please?" A forlorn Libba
was worrisome.

"Of course." The dogs and I followed her outside and

watched as she picked a chair at the wrought-iron table and lit a cigarette.

One of my neighbors was barbequing and the delicious aroma of slow-cooking brisket hung heavy in the humid air.

My stomach rumbled like a freight train.

"Wow. Hungry?"

"Sorry. I missed lunch. Now, talk."

"I'm not in the mood reveal my secrets."

"What secrets?"

"I have secrets."

"Yeah, right. We've known each other our whole lives. I know all your secrets."

"You'd be surprised. Can we drop it? Please? Tell me about your day." Libba tilted her head toward the sky and blew a plume of smoke. "What happened?"

I relented. "Mother found out I sent the kids to Aunt Sis instead of her."

She gaped at me over the rim of her glass. "Yikes."

I could think of stronger words. "She's not speaking to me."

She blew another plume. "Silver lining?"

I joined her at the table. My chair still retained the heat from an afternoon spent baking in the sun, and I tugged at my hem, pulling so the linen of my dress protected the back of my legs. "I took a Bundt to Gib Miles."

She sat straighter, suddenly hyper-alert despite who-knew-how-many martinis. "Gib has Bundt cake?"

"It's probably gone by now. There was a crowd."

She frowned. "Can't she make extras?"

"The last thing I need in this house is Bundt cake."

"Wrong. The last thing you need is another dog."

My dogs gave her reproachful stares.

She ignored them. "What happened at Gib's?"

"He wanted advice on talking to his children."

"Not fun," she allowed. "But still better than listening to him sob about Audrey or confess that he killed her.

"Silver linings," I replied dryly. "While I was there, I ran into Helen Phelps. Literally. I almost knocked her down. The poor woman is a mess."

"Over Baxter?"

"No, because the Royals lost last night." A bad day plus good gin equaled sarcasm.

"Did they?"

"How would I know? Of course, over Baxter. She must have really loved him. Then came the *pièce de résistance*. Sandy Wilcox."

"Oh, no." Libba looked suitably horrified. "What did she want?"

"Grant got caught in a lie, which she repeated to me before she knew it was a lie. Then he made her tell me it was all a misunderstanding."

"He's cheating on her?"

"That's my guess."

"And she refuses to see it." Libba swirled her gin. "Sometimes a woman refuses to see the truth, even when it's jumping up and down in front of her, begging for her attention. You can't change that."

"I know. I know. But I still want to give Grant a piece of my mind."

"What good would that do? It won't rip off Sandy's blinders. It won't change Grant's behavior." She tapped her cigarette in the ashtray I kept outside for her use. "Nothing but wasted words."

"It might make me feel better."

"Doubtful. You'd be frustrated at his lack of remorse." Libba, who's had the foresight to bring the martini pitcher with her, refilled our glasses. "Anything else?"

"The usual. Finn got away from me on our morning walk and I had to chase him through Fairway. Frank is still following me."

Libba put down her the pitcher and stared at me. "Who is Frank?"

I hadn't told her? "He's in the mob," I whispered.

"What did you say?" She couldn't hear me. The locusts were too loud. So loud I could probably fire a gun and no one would hear it.

I raised my voice and repeated, "He's in the mob."

"A mobster is following you?" Libba wasn't the pearl-clutching type, but her hand moved to her throat.

"Yes."

"Now?"

"Maybe."

"So, he could be outside, sitting in his car, watching the house?"

"Possibly. Sometimes I can spot him. Sometimes I can't. I don't know if it's because he's not there or really good at hiding."

She stood. "We should invite him in for a drink."

"Sit down," I barked. "Frank isn't Al Pacino. This isn't *The Godfather*. Frank is scary. He's the reason we sent the kids to Sis."

"Why is he following you?"

"To ensure that Anarchy finds the real killer. Frank swears the mob didn't kill Baxter. I think he'll follow me till we find the real killer."

"He's truly scary?"

"Terrifying," I confirmed.

"Then we need to figure out who did it. Who had a motive?"

"Helen. But she has an alibi. She didn't leave her house on Thursday night."

"Remind me where she lives."

"Just off Overhill. Big Tudor."

"That's right. I remember now. She hosted a DAR meeting last year. Who else?"

"Well…it sounds crazy, but..."

"What?"

"Honoria Miller says—"

Libba held up her hand, stopping me. "We haven't even talked about that party. Everyone's talking and I want details." "Just your average brawl over a four-karat diamond. They're lucky; no royal Danica was broken."

"Four karats?"

"At least."

She whistled, then slapped at a mosquito. At least I hoped it was a mosquito. If not, she was crazy, too.

"According to Aunt Sis, Honoria thinks Donna may have killed Morton's first wife. Also, she thinks Donna isn't Donna."

Libba frowned at me. "I've already had two martinis. You're going to have to explain that."

"Honoria thinks that the Donna we've met stole a woman named Donna Barksdale's identity."

"Honoria is almost as crazy as her daughter-in-law."

"The real Donna graduated from Miami of Ohio in 1952."

"So?"

"That's the same year Baxter graduated from there. What if he knew Donna stole another woman's name?"

"She killed him and made it look like a mob hit?"

I drank. Deeply. In the afternoon heat, the cold gin tasted heavenly. "It's crazy."

"We've seen crazier." Sadly, she wasn't wrong. "Anyone else?"

"Lloyd Crowder," I admitted with reluctance.

She wrinkled her nose. "Lloyd's too boring to be a killer."

"And Baxter was too boring to go to sex clubs."

"Touché. Why Lloyd?"

"He says that whatever he and Baxter discussed over drinks is privileged."

"And?"

"Who discusses private matters at the bar at Nabil's. The whole world walks by."

"Do you think he's Audrey's other lover?"

I gaped at my friend. Sometimes she astonished me with her brilliance. "Maybe we've been looking at this the wrong way. What if Audrey's the primary victim, and Baxter was caught in the crossfire?"

"Then why move Baxter's body?"

I took another sip of my martini. A small one, I was already feeling the alcohol. "Go with me on this."

"Okay, who wanted Audrey dead? Gib?"

"I don't think so. Gib adores his children, and he's genuinely worried how their mother's death will affect them."

"Then who?"

"Audrey had a second partner. Maybe he got jealous." We really needed to get that name from Kathleen Mahoney. Or maybe we already had it. Maybe, Audrey's other lover was Lloyd Crowder. "We need to talk to Elizabeth."

"You mean go to her house?"

"I do."

"Now?" Libba shook her head. "We've been drinking. We can't drive."

"Then we'll walk. It's only a few blocks."

"It's hot out."

I was aware. She'd dragged into the heat so she could smoke. "We can't drive." I used her words against her.

"We can go tomorrow."

"The sooner we catch the killer, the sooner Frank stops following me, and the sooner the kids can come home."

"Hey! Do you suppose he'd give us a ride?"

"No! A million times 'no.' He. Is. Scary."

"So you say." She crushed out her cigarette, then held up her glass. "But we'll need roadies."

I clutched the edge of the table, using it to rise to my feet. When had the world gone wobbly?

Libba, whose tolerance for alcohol far exceeded mine, stood gracefully.

We went to the kitchen, where I found her a plastic cup.

"You're not having one?"

"I've had enough."

She shook her head as if I was a sore disappointment, filled the cup, then stashed the pitcher in the fridge. "For later."

Then, sticking to the shady side of the street, we walked to Elizabeth's house.

"What are you going to say?" Libba asked as we staggered up the front walk. "You can't just ask Elizabeth if Lloyd was carrying on with Audrey."

"That doesn't seem like a good plan."

"Then what?"

"I'll figure it out when we're in there." I jabbed at the doorbell.

A moment later, the door swung open.

Elizabeth smiled and tilted her head, clearly surprised by our arrival, but too polite to say it. "Ellison, Libba, how lovely to see you."

"We were in the neighborhood," Libba replied.

I elbowed her. We were always in the neighborhood. We *lived* in the neighborhood. At least I did. If she married Charlie, she would, too. "Traveling cocktails," I blurted. "We're having traveling cocktails." I stole the cup from Libba's hand and drank.

"Ellison has had a rough day," Libba explained.

"I can relate," Elizabeth replied. "What are you drinking?"

Libba stole the cup back. The empty cup. "We were drinking martinis."

"Sounds like you need a refill. Come on in."

Elizabeth led us to her living room, which was blessedly cool after the late afternoon heat. "Sit. I'll be back in two shakes."

Libba sank into a club chair.

I perused the art on the walls, pausing in front of a Rothko in shades of cerulean and hansa yellow. "Gorgeous."

"Isn't it?" Elizabeth stood in the living room's entrance holding a tray.

I spotted a martini pitcher and three glasses. Hopefully Elizabeth used more vermouth than Libba. If not, they'd need to call a cab to get me home.

"I hope you don't mind. I like them dirty." Elizabeth poured and handed the glass to Libba.

Libba sipped and sighed. "Perfection."

"Here's yours, Ellison."

I accepted a glass and sipped. The martini was very dirty. I tasted olives and vermouth and said a silent thank you. "Delicious."

Elizabeth poured herself a glass, then claimed the club chair that matched Libba's. "Now, tell me, what made your day so rotten?"

"There's a mobster following her around," Libba replied.

"Now?" Elizabeth glanced out the front window.

"No. Not now." Libba sounded so sure. As if she'd spent the walk over here glancing over her shoulder. Now that I thought about it, she had. "It's because of Baxter's death."

"Were Baxter and Lloyd friends?" Had I asked her that before? I couldn't remember.

Elizabeth tilted her head, considering her answer. "Not particularly. When Lloyd mentioned that Baxter wanted to meet him for a drink, I thought it was strange. And poor Lloyd, he's been so busy. A large corporation wants to acquire one of his client's companies, and he's been chained to the office. But, you know my husband. Such a good man. Of course he said 'yes' when Baxter asked." She flushed. "I was his out."

"His out?" asked Libba.

"I showed up for dinner and dragged Lloyd away from the bar. You know the rest. Baxter left."

The kernel of a brilliant idea floated on the sea of gin sloshing around in my brain. I perched on the edge of the couch and, with exaggerated care, placed the glass on the coffee table.

Elizabeth frowned. "You don't like it?"

"I do," I assured her. "I'm pacing myself. Now, please tell me about your Rothko."

CHAPTER EIGHTEEN

"The next time you decide to cocktail your way through the neighborhood, let me know. I'll join you." Elizabeth ushered us outside.

The sun seemed far too bright, and I wished I'd remembered my sunglasses.

"We will," Libba promised. "But only if you promise to mix a pitcher of martinis for the roadies."

"It's a deal." Elizabeth waved us goodbye.

As soon our feet hit the sidewalk, Libba turned on me. "What the heck, Ellison? I thought you were going to ask her about Lloyd and Audrey."

"I had a better idea."

She squinted at me. "To talk about art?"

"Obviously not. How well do you know the bartender at Nabil's?"

"Tommy? Cute boy. He makes a mean Manhattan."

"You're on a first-name basis?"

"Yeah." She made the one-syllable word last for three. Libba was on a first-named basis with plenty of bartenders. The real question was why I wasn't.

Easy answer? I didn't drink like a fish. "We need to go. Now."

She frowned at me. "To Nabil's? Why?"

"Because, even if whatever Baxter and Lloyd discussed is privileged. What Tommy may have overheard is not."

A slow smile curled her lips. "Even drunk, you're smart."

"I'm not drunk." I tripped on a sidewalk crack, and only Libba's quick reflexes kept me from sprawling. How did she *do* that? By my count she'd had at least three martinis. I'd had barely two, and the world was muzzy.

"You were telling me how you're not drunk?" Her smirk was the definition of obnoxious.

"Oh, shut up."

She snickered. "Maybe a glass of water before we catch a cab to the Plaza."

Thirty minutes later, we perched on stools at Nabil's dark, cool bar. The heat, the humidity, and the too-bright sun seemed a million miles away. I smelled something delicious coming from the kitchen—something with garlic and onions—and my mouth watered.

"Hey, Tommy."

"Libba, nice to see you." Tommy, who was young, handsome, and knew it, offered her a charming smile. "The usual?"

"Please. My lightweight friend will have a seltzer and lime."

We watched as Tommy combined rye, bitters and sweet vermouth. Then he added a cherry. The seltzer and lime took less effort.

"Thanks." Libba lifted her glass in his direction.

"You're welcome." He started to turn away, but she stopped him.

"We have a question for you."

He looked at her expectantly.

"Do you know Baxter Phelps or Lloyd Crowder?" I asked.

He nodded slowly. "Mr. Crowder is a regular."

"Do remember when you last saw him?"

"He was in last Thursday. Met another man for drinks. They sat where you're sitting. Same two stools."

"Did you hear what they were talking about?" My hand hit my glass, and seltzer sloshed on the bar.

Tommy wiped away the mess with a bar towel. "I can't be sure, but I got the impression the man I didn't know—Baxter Phelps, you said—had some information that could mess up a deal Mr. Crowder had been working on."

My heart beat a little faster. "Oh?"

"They got agitated." Tommy surveyed the length of the bar, then he leaned forward, and we were assaulted by a cloud of Aramis. "It had something to do with family values and a sex club," he whispered.

Did all roads lead to Club K?

Libba grinned like the Cheshire Cat. "Did you hear any names?"

Tommy frowned as if our lack of shock disappointed him. "No."

"You're sure?" Libba slipped a twenty across the bar.

He eyed the bill with regret. "There was a guy at the end of the bar who wanted to chat, so I only heard bits and pieces of Mr. Crowder's conversation."

That was a crying shame.

Libba pushed the twenty closer to him, then withdrew her hand.

Tommy pocketed the bill.

I'd have to repay her later. "Did you get the idea that Baxter was threatening Mr. Crowder?"

"No. But Mr. Crowder wasn't happy. He said the other guy would pay if he blew up the deal."

Things weren't looking good for Lloyd.

Then again, Lloyd was a lawyer. "Paying" might mean a long, expensive lawsuit.

"What else can you tell us?"

"Hold on." Tommy hurried to the other end of the bar to take someone's order.

"What do you think?" Libba asked.

"I don't think Lloyd was having an affair with Audrey."

"Agreed. We need to find out more about this deal."

"Maybe Anarchy can get a subpoena for Lloyd's client list." Even as I suggested it, I knew it was a longshot. "Family values and a sex club?"

"I know." Libba took a sip of her Manhattan, then lit a cigarette. "I don't get it."

I resigned myself to smelling like an ashtray. "Someone from a family-values oriented company was visiting Club K?"

"That's enough to blow up a whole deal?"

"The other guy ran out on his tab. Mr. Crowder picked it up." Tommy had returned.

Interesting, but not helpful. "Did you hear the name of the company?"

"Nah."

"Who mentioned the sex club first?" I asked.

"I think it was the other guy. Must have been. Mr. Crowder looked gobsmacked." He chuckled. "I expected you two to look the same."

"It takes a lot to shock us," said Libba. "Especially Ellison."

Tommy gazed at me with interest. I could almost see the cogs turning in his bartender brain. He was wondering if I frequented sex clubs.

I refrained from kicking Libba in the shin. Barely. "Libba will give you her number in case you think of anything else."

"I will? Why don't you give him yours?"

I looked Tommy in the eye, and he winked at me. Oh dear Lord. "I'm not giving Tommy my number because my police officer husband wouldn't like it."

Tommy gulped. "I've already got your number, Libba. If I

think of anything else, I'll call." He slid away, pretending the customer at the end of the bar had called him.

"You should have flirted," Libba groused. "You never know what he might have remembered."

"I'm married. I'm not flirting with anyone but Anarchy."

"Right, there is a reason to stay single."

"No." I wagged my finger at her. "No, no, no. I am not giving you reason to change your mind about Charlie."

Libba scowled into her empty glass. "Should we order another round?"

I glanced at my watch. Were the kids back from rafting? "I need to get home. Where's your car?" Not that she should be driving, but I did wonder how she got to my house.

"Charlie's. My car is at Charlie's."

"So you were at Charlie's, and you decided to drink at my house instead."

"The housekeeper was there, and she's a little judgy, so I decided to walk over."

"We wouldn't want any judgment."

"No." Libba gave me the stink eye. "We would not."

ANARCHY WAS AT HOME WHEN I GOT THERE. I FOUND HIM ON THE couch in the den, nursing a finger of scotch.

I bent down and kissed his cheek. "Hi, there."

"Hi. Where have you been?"

"Libba and I went for a drink."

"The pitcher of martinis in the fridge wasn't good enough?"

"Actually, it wasn't. We were at Nabil's." I recounted everything Tommy had told us.

He leaned his head against the back of the sofa. "I'll have to talk to him. It sounds as if Lloyd is being overly generous when he says his conversation with Baxter was privileged."

I hadn't thought of that. "How was your day?"

"I spent four hours with Kathleen Mahoney."

Words no woman wanted to hear. "Did she give you a name?"

"She did not. She's decided she can't recall who Audrey met on weekends."

"That's a big fat lie."

"I know, but there's nothing I can do about it."

"Did you find out anything more about Donna Miller?"

"No. But that reminds me. Marilyn Tremblay called for you."

"That poor woman. Should I call her now?"

He pulled me onto the couch. "Give it a few minutes."

I rested my head on his shoulder. He smelled of sunshine and the cologne I'd bought him for his birthday. "I wish there was something we could do to get Kathleen to talk." I was certain Audrey's second partner was the key to everything. "Did you tell her he might be a killer?"

"I did. She doesn't care."

"What else can we do?"

He shook his head, then dropped a kiss on my forehead. "If you figure anything out, let me know. What?"

"What?"

"You stiffened."

"Did I?" There was no way I was telling my by-the-book-rule-following husband the idea that had flitted through my brain. Not, yet. Not when it was a longshot. "I didn't mean to. Just pondering ways to get Kathleen to talk. I'm assuming I can't point a gun at her?"

"Ha. What are we doing for dinner?"

"Aggie left chicken salad."

"Let's go out."

"Where?"

His fingers played with a strand of my hair. "Your choice."

"The Golden Ox." The Golden Ox was a Kansas City institution. Built near the American Royal and next to what used to be the stockyards, the restaurant was one of the best steakhouses in town.

"You want steak?"

"Why not?" I didn't add there was a sign in the West Bottoms I wanted to read.

~

You're sure you want to do this? It was rare that Mr. Coffee questioned my judgment.

"I'm sure."

Anarchy might not like it.

"The kids start school in a week. We need to get them home."

I notice you waited until he left for work before you called.

"I manage my own money." I topped off my coffee mug and glanced at my watch. I had plenty of time. My appointment wasn't until ten.

This isn't about money.

Mr. Coffee was right, but I didn't see any other options. I wanted to stop looking over my shoulder to see if Frank was there. More importantly, I wanted my kids back.

I headed upstairs and dressed carefully. The same conservative-yet-chic dress I'd worn to Baxter's funeral, low-heeled pumps, and a navy Gucci purse I bought when Anarchy and I were on our honeymoon. Then I glanced at my watch. I had plenty of time to swing by the bank before my appointment.

At precisely ten o'clock I breezed into the well-appointed offices of Keller and Coben.

The receptionist looked up from perusing the morning paper. "May I help you?"

"Ellison Jones to see Mr. Coben."

She picked up the phone. "I'll tell him you're here, Ms. Jones."

"Thank you." I moved toward the waiting room. A wall of windows offered a view to the west. We were up high enough that I had a clear view of Kansas City, Kansas.

"Would you care for coffee?"

"Please. With cream if you've got it."

She nodded as she spoke into the phone. "Ms. Jones to see you, sir."

I settled into a leather club chair and picked up a magazine about commercial real estate, idly flipping through its pages.

"Your coffee." The receptionist put a mug on the table next to me. "Mr. Coben will see you in a few minutes."

Mr. Coben kept me waiting for thirty. And by the time the receptionist, whose name was Nancy, lead me to his office, I was seriously annoyed. I doubted if he'd have kept Mr. Jones waiting so long.

Michael Coben stood when I entered his office. The man was short and stocky, bald as a billiard ball, and projected a why-are-you-taking-up-my-time-little-lady attitude. "Ms. Jones, a pleasure to meet you. How may I help you, today?"

"It's Mrs. Jones."

"My mistake." He looked chagrined, not contrite, as if he didn't appreciate having a woman correct him.

Without invitation, I took the chair across from his. "You have properties for sale in the West Bottoms."

He steepled his fingers and looked down his fleshy nose. "We do."

I pulled out a slip of paper with an address written on it and slid it across his desk. "This property?"

He gave a brief nod. "I believe so, yes."

"I'd like to buy it."

He blinked. "That property is on the market for a three-hundred-fifty-thousand dollars, Mrs. Jones."

"Alright." I wasn't here to haggle. I opened my handbag and pulled out my checkbook.

"I can't just take a check."

"I know. I'm sure there are contracts to sign."

"And inspections."

"Not necessary. I'll buy the building as is. And, I'll pay an extra dollar per square foot if we can close this afternoon."

"You don't understand, Mrs. Jones." Lord, have mercy, could a man sound more patronizing? "There's the financing—"

I reached into my handbag a second time, then slid a guarantee of funds from our bank across his desk.

He gulped. "You can spend up to a million dollars."

"I'm aware of my budget, Mr. Coben."

"There are better buildings."

"I want that one."

"I need to speak with the current owner."

"I'll wait."

"But...I..." the man was flustered.

I smiled sweetly and crossed my ankles.

Four hours later, I was the owner of a twenty-six-thousand square foot warehouse in the West Bottoms.

Four hours and fifteen minutes later, I knocked on its door and asked to see Kathleen Mahoney.

"Seersucker, you're back." Kathleen, who only kept me waiting ten minutes, wore a red leather bustier and skin-tight black pants. She licked her ruby lips, and added, "Your husband can't get enough of me either."

I gave her a tight smile.

"Anarchy and I spent hours together on Saturday."

"He told me."

"Did he?" She practically purred. She definitely smirked.

I couldn't wait to erase that smirk. "I tried something new today."

"Oh?"

"Mhmm. I bought a building." I looked around Kathleen's dungeon with my eyes narrowed, appraising, almost like I was measuring for drapes. "This building."

"You did not."

"I did. Would you like to see the contract? I'm your new landlord." I'd done it. I'd wiped the superior expression off her face. Inside, I completed a perfect cartwheel.

"You bought a sex club."

"I bought a building. These old warehouses have such great light. I bet the upper floor would make a fabulous studio for me. I can rent studio space on the other floors to other artists."

She crossed her arms. "What do you want?"

"I think you know."

Her lips pursed. Her eyes closed. Her hands fisted. And, for a few long, long seconds, I worried I'd spent nearly four-hundred-thousand dollars for nothing.

"Grant Wilcox. Audrey's other partner was Grant Wilcox."

CHAPTER NINETEEN

"Anarchy?" My voice carried throughout the downstairs.

Aggie stepped into the front hall. Today's kaftan was sunflower yellow and dotted with brown mushrooms. "He took the dogs for a walk."

I felt a twinge of disappointment. I couldn't wait to tell him about Grant Wilcox. "How long has he been gone?"

She glanced at her watch. "Twenty minutes. Marilyn Tremblay has called twice."

"I'll call her. Anyone else?"

"Your aunt. She said to tell you they're taking the kids on a long trail ride and not to worry if you can't reach them." Aggie took in my outfit. "Another funeral?"

"Not today. Today, I bought a building." I lifted my chin and pretended I did things like that all the time.

"Where?"

"The West Bottoms."

She frowned. "Isn't that in a flood plain?"

"When the river crests too high." The West Bottoms had suffered several catastrophic floods. I didn't care.

"Aren't most of the buildings down there warehouses?"

I nodded, barely suppressing my absolute glee. Putting Michael Coben in his place had been so empowering. Maybe I needed to buy more buildings. I could be the kingpin—queenpin —of the West Bottoms. "They are."

"And you bought one?"

I couldn't contain my grin. "I did."

"Why a warehouse?"

"Leverage. That reminds me, I need to call Hunter Tafft." I planned on asking him to set up a holding company that could take ownership of the warehouse. I did not want my name on the title of a building that housed a sex club.

Aggie's brows lifted. "Leverage?"

"I got a name from Kathleen Mahoney." Getting Grant's name from her was even better than signing the real estate contract.

"You bought a warehouse to get a name?"

"I did."

"You're clearly pleased as punch."

"I think I have the killer's name, and I want this case solved so we can bring Grace and Beau home from Colorado."

"Amen to that."

Together, we walked toward the kitchen.

"I'm making salmon for dinner."

"Sounds delicious. Although…"

"Detective Jones may be working," she finished for me.

Tonight, a missed dinner wouldn't bother me in the least. "I guess I should call Marilyn."

"Would you like anything to drink?"

The thought of liquor made my stomach cramp. "Iced tea, please."

"I'll bring it you."

I headed for the den and settled behind my desk. Then, I stretched my legs and laced my fingers behind my head. I'd done it. Me. I'd forced a commercial real estate sale in record time, then I'd made Kathleen give me Grant's name.

Grant.

My upper lip curled just thinking about him. He was a liar and a cheater and most likely a murderer. I wouldn't miss him or his padded toilet seats.

"Your tea." Aggie put the glass on my desk.

"Thank you," I told her. Then I looked up Marilyn's number and dialed.

"Tremblay residence." It was a man's voice.

"May I please speak with Marilyn?"

"May I tell her who's calling?"

"Ellison Jones."

"Ellison, it's Byron. If you'll hold the line, I'll get Marilyn."

"Of course."

He put down the phone, and I took a moment to savor the memory of Michael Coben's face when I handed him my letter of credit.

"Ellison?"

"Marilyn, how are you? How's Emma?"

"We're all still in shock."

"I bet."

"Honoria has invited us for dinner tomorrow night."

"Are you going?"

"I don't know. Part of me thinks she set up that awful scene on purpose."

All of me thought that. "Is Emma going to marry Price?"

"Yes." That one word carried anger and worry and the tiniest bit of hope. "She loves him. He took her to a lawyer today and they're going to request a restraining order. Donna will never get near Emma again."

That would make holidays loads of fun. "What does Morton have to say about his wife's behavior?"

"Emma says he was on the phone for most of the day with a

lawyer in Boston. They're still residents of Massachusetts so he'll have to file for divorce there." That solved the uncomfortable Christmas problem.

"So Honoria won."

"I suspect Honoria always wins."

"I suspect you're right. In which case, you'd better join her for dinner."

"The invitation includes you and Anarchy."

Oh, dear Lord. "Why?"

"You made an impression. Please, say you'll join us. I need a friend there.

"What does Byron say about all this?"

"He wants Emma to return the ring and cut off contact. He says trailer trash shows better behavior."

He wasn't wrong. "Where and when?"

"The American at seven."

"We'll be there. Or, I'll be there. If something breaks on Anarchy's case, he may have to send his regrets."

"Thank you." Her gratitude was evident.

The dogs raced into the den and crowded around my desk, demanding pets.

"Marilyn, Anarchy just got home. I need to go."

"Go," she replied. "I'll see you tomorrow."

I hurried into the kitchen, where Anarchy stood next to the sink, drinking a glass of water.

"Guess what?" A grin stretched across my whole face.

He quirked a brow. "What?"

"Guess!"

"There was a sale at Swanson's."

"No. I got the name."

He pushed off the counter. "For Audrey's other lover? How?"

This was the dicey part. "We now own a warehouse."

He put his glass down and stared at me. "You bought Kathleen's building?"

"It wasn't her building. It belonged to a man named Cyrus Banks. She just rents space there. Now, it's ours." Mine. I thought it best not to Anarchy's name on the title to a building that housed a sex club.

"How?"

"I went to see the real estate broker, offered cash, and paid a bonus if we could settle today. The building has been on the market for two years. Mr. Banks was thrilled to oblige me."

"Then you threatened Kathleen?"

"Not at all. I just told her how perfect the space would be for artists' studios."

"We own a sex club."

"We own a building," I corrected. "I'll get Hunter to fix that tomorrow."

"Fix that how?"

"We'll shift ownership to a holding company. Now, about that name—"

He grimaced. "We're not done talking about the warehouse."

"Don't you want to go and arrest Audrey's lover?" I paused for dramatic effect. "It's Grant Wilcox."

His eyes widened. "You're kidding?"

"I am not. That's the name Kathleen gave me."

"I have to bring him in for questioning."

"I expected nothing less."

"Aggie told me she's grilling salmon." Regret tinged his voice.

"We'll save you some." I lifted onto my toes and kissed his cheek. "Go get a confession. Then, we can bring the kids home."

～

WOOF!

I rolled over and looked at the clock. Five minutes till midnight.

Woof!

"Hush, Finn." Anarchy's voice carried up the stairs and through our open bedroom door.

I swung my feet to the floor, pulled on a robe, and hurried downstairs.

Anarchy stood at the backdoor watching the dogs as they sniffed for any critter foolish enough to encroach on their territory.

"You're home."

He turned. "Did I wake you?"

"Finn."

"Sorry about that."

"Did he confess?"

"No."

My shoulders slumped. In my mind, Grant had blabbed about brutally killing two people. "What did he say about Club K?"

"He admits to going there. He even admits that he had a relationship with Audrey. But he insists that cheating on his wife isn't a crime."

He was right about that. "You look tired." More than tired, Anarchy looked gray beneath his tan.

"How much did you spend on that building?"

"Four hundred thousand. Why?"

He scrubbed his palms over his face. "I don't think he did it."

"Did you let him go?"

"We're holding him, but I'm not sure the prosecutor will file charges."

I wrapped my arms across my chest. "How could that be? He doesn't have an alibi."

"And we don't have any evidence."

"But he has a motive."

"What's the motive, Ellison?"

"He was jealous about Baxter's relationship with Audrey."

"He says it's the other way around. Baxter was jealous of him."

"But Baxter is the one who was murdered." I studied my husband. "You look dead on your feet. Go upstairs and get ready for bed. I'll let the dogs in."

That he didn't argue, spoke volumes. Without a word, he trudged up the back stairs.

I gave the dogs a few minutes, then opened the door and called, "Treats."

They raced toward me, and I gave each of them a biscuit. "Go back to bed."

They danced around as if they were at a midnight party.

"I mean it. Bed." When it was just Max, he slept in our room. Finn liked sleeping downstairs, and Max had taken to staying with him. "Now." Not waiting to see if they complied, I climbed the stairs after my husband.

He was already in his pajamas when I reached our bedroom. But he wasn't in bed. Instead, he sat in the chair be the window with a file open on his lap.

"Bed," I told him. Then, I pointed at our comfortable mattress. "Now. Nothing will change between now and tomorrow morning, and you need some rest."

"You spent a fortune on a building."

"I'd do it again in a heartbeat."

"But—"

"No, buts. Get some sleep."

My husband climbed into bed and his eyes quickly fluttered shut.

I wasn't so lucky. A single thought chased its tail in my brain. If Anarchy was right, if Grant hadn't killed Baxter and Audrey, who had?

CHAPTER TWENTY

M r. Coffee and I sat in companionable silence.
I sipped.
He kept the coffee warm.

You look tired.

There was a lot of that going around.

Do you need a warmup?

I stared into my near-empty cup. "I do." I got up and refilled. To the brim.

The kitchen clock read seven o'clock, and Anarchy was already gone. I hoped, fresh from several hours sleep, he'd make more progress getting a confession from Grant.

Ding dong.

"What on earth?" No one came calling this early. I pulled my robe closer around me, then tightened the sash.

Ding dong.

Unconscionably early and impatient? Quite the combination.

The dogs and I hurried to the front door.

"Ellison, I need to talk to you. Now!" Sandy Wilcox was on my front stoop.

With a sigh that reached my toes, I opened the door.

Graceful, willowy Sandy didn't look so elegant this morning. Her hair was unkempt and yesterday's mascara smudged the skin beneath her eyes. At least I hoped it was mascara. If not, she had serious, concerning dark circles. "They've arrested Grant."

"How about some coffee?" Coffee might not solve problems, but it did make them more manageable.

"You have to tell your husband that Grant is innocent. He'd never kill anyone."

"If he's innocent, he has nothing to worry about."

"You don't understand." She shook her head. Violently. "We can't afford even a whiff of scandal. Anarchy needs to let him go. Immediately.

"Sandy, come inside. Have a cup of coffee and tell me what's wrong."

"Your husband arrested mine!" She was loud enough that anyone out walking before the heat became oppressive, even if they were blocks away, probably heard her.

"Come inside." I opened the door wider. "We'll talk this out."

She followed me into the kitchen, and I poured her a mug. "Cream or sugar?"

"Black."

When her fingers wrapped around the mug, I asked, "What's this about a scandal?"

"Grant is selling his company to Faith Industries. That's why we went to San Francisco. To meet with the chief executive officer and board president. Grant never takes me on business trips, but they wanted to meet me. They're all about family values." She raked her fingers through her messy hair. "There have been so many meetings, and phone calls, and lawyers. And the one thing that has been impressed upon us again and again is their morals clause."

Whoopsie. That might be a problem. "Who's representing Grant?"

"Lloyd Crowder. He's been wonderful. Rather than charging us an hourly rate, we worked out a deal where he got a percentage."

If Baxter had gone public about Grant's trips to Club K, the deal would have fallen apart and all the hours that Lloyd had put in would have been for nothing. Worse than nothing. Non-billable hours.

It was a strong motive for murder. But Elizabeth said she'd spent the evening with her husband, and I believed her.

The motive was equally strong for Grant. If Baxter revealed that Grant cheated on Sandy at a kinky sex club, Faith Industries would walk—no, they'd run.

Both scenarios explained Baxter's death, but not Audrey's. Had someone followed him to her house? I closed my eyes and tried to find a reason for Audrey's death.

"Ellison!" Sandy shrieked.

I blinked. "What?"

"You were a million miles away, and I need your help." She was pacing between the door to the yard and the island.

Max, who'd proven himself time and again to be a good judge of character, watched her carefully.

"Sandy, I don't know what to tell you." *Grant cheated on you with Audrey Miles at a sex club in the West Bottoms.* Sandy held tight to her blinders. Telling her the truth wouldn't get me anywhere. It might even get me hurt.

I regretted letting her into my house.

"Say something!"

That morals clause is a killer, and your deal is dead in the water. Probably not that. "Anarchy is an excellent detective. If Grant is innocent, he has nothing to worry about."

"He. Was. Arrested!"

I glanced at Mr. Coffee. He was marvelous about providing coffee and advice and lending a sympathetic ear. When it came to possibly crazy, possibly dangerous, women in the kitchen, he was no help.

Are you sure she's not the killer?

Oh, dear Lord. She wouldn't be the first angry wife to kill her husband's mistress. And Baxter had threatened the sale of Grant's company.

"Call your husband," she insisted. "Tell him Grant is innocent. Tell him to let Grant go."

"Okay." My tone was placating. I picked up the phone and dialed.

"Jones."

"It's me. Sandy Wilcox is here with me."

She grabbed my arm and shook me till my teeth rattled. "Tell him!"

Next to me, Max growled. Finn whined softly.

"Sandy wants me to tell you that Grant is innocent."

"Are you safe?" His voice was edged with worry.

"I don't know."

"Sending a squad car. Try to keep her calm."

That ship had sailed.

"Tell him to let Grant go!"

"She wants you to release Grant."

"Yeah, I heard that."

"Let me talk to him." Sandy held out her hand for the receiver.

"I'm putting Sandy on the line."

She clutched the phone tightly. "Anarchy, Grant didn't kill those people. You have to let him go."

She pressed the receiver against her ear and nodded, then her expression cleared. "Thank you. Thank you so much."

I kept my mouth firmly shut. There was no way—no way—Anarchy was releasing Grant just because his deranged wife asked. She hadn't even asked nicely. No. My husband was worried for my safety and was telling her what she wanted to hear.

I moved away from her, putting the kitchen island between us and discreetly opening Aggie's knife drawer.

Sandy hung up and beamed at me. "He'll let Grant go."

"That's wonderful news."

Her smile flickered. "I expected he'd put up an argument."

"He worked all night. Maybe he found some exculpatory evidence."

"What's that?"

"Evidence that proves Grant is innocent." I kept ahold of the small kitchen knife.

Finn joined me on the far side of the island. Max did not. He positioned himself between Sandy and me.

"He said they'd send a squad car to pick me up."

Anarchy was a genius.

"The car will take me to the station, then Grant and I can go home."

"Wonderful news." A good hostess would have taken the opportunity to offer her more coffee. But my hands were full. One held my mug. The other held a knife. And I wasn't letting go of either. "How did you get here?" I hadn't noticed a car when I opened the front door.

"I walked. It's not far, and I felt too upset to drive. I feel so relieved. Thank heavens Anarchy saw reason. I just can't stand the thought of Grant being in jail. I paced the floor all night." Either Sandy was the best actress I'd ever met or she hadn't killed Baxter and Audrey.

If Anarchy was right, and Grant was innocent, that left Lloyd and Donna.

And Lloyd had an alibi.

I tried to wrap my head around Donna Miller, with her perfectly coiffed hair and Chanel suits, shooting Baxter. And I couldn't.

"Ellison!"

"What?"

"You keep doing that, disappearing into your head."

"I'm sorry. Now that we know Grant is innocent—" I remained unconvinced "—I'm wondering who killed Baxter and Audrey."

"Helen."

"Helen has an alibi."

"She's smart. She could have faked it."

One couldn't fake a car that never left the driveway.

Ding dong.

My death grip on the kitchen knife loosened. "I bet that's your ride. After you." I waved Sandy to the front hall. She might have calmed down, but that didn't mean I wanted her behind me.

Moments later, the uniformed officer led Sandy to the back of the squad car.

"I can't ride back there like a criminal."

"I'm sorry, ma'am, it's against regulations for you to ride in front."

He closed the door on her, then turned and said, "Detective Jones is on his way home."

"Thank you, officer." I retreated inside, locked the doors, and returned to the kitchen where I refilled my coffee mug.

"You were both very brave." I handed out dog biscuits. Whole ones.

The dogs wagged their stubby tails.

Then I sank onto a stool and sipped coffee like my life depended on it. "Why is it I attract the crazies?"

I wish I had a good answer. You handled her well.

"Most of that was Anarchy."

He's on his way?

"Should be here any minute." I turned as the backdoor flew open.

"Ellison?"

"I'm here. I'm fine."

He wrapped me in a bear hug. "Why did you let her in?"

"I didn't know she was coo coo." I tilted my head so I could see his handsome face. "Lloyd Crowder is representing Grant in the sale of his company. They're selling to a corporation called Faith Industries. There's a morals clause."

"Baxter threatened to reveal Grant's trips to Club K and tank the sale." A small smile graced his lips. "That's a motive the prosecutor might believe." His hands ran up and down my arms. "You're sure you're okay?"

"I'm fine. I think she was mostly harmless." Maybe.

Had Frank had seen the officer loading Sandy into the cruiser? Was that enough proof that Anarchy was pursuing other leads? "You should go back to the station. Take another run at Grant."

He pursed his lips. "What are you going to do, today?"

"I'm going to call Hunter about transferring the ownership of the warehouse."

"Ellison, you spent four-hundred-thousand dollars." His expression was half-dazed, half-worried.

I shrugged. "Give or take."

"Can we afford that?"

"My father's mother was from Texas. Her father was an oilman. She inherited his wells, them left them to Marjorie and me."

"I didn't realize I was marrying an heiress."

"There's such a thing as too much money. It destroys children. Aside from the shopping and a few trips, I try to live as if the oil wells don't exist. I've certainly never done anything like buying a building."

"You're amazing." He brushed a soft kiss across my lips, then pulled away with apparent reluctance. "I should go."

I held up my crossed fingers. "With any luck, we can bring the kids home tomorrow."

CHAPTER TWENTY-ONE

I gave the dogs my attention. They'd been circling the entire time I was on the phone with Hunter. Now that I'd hung up, they were perfectly happy to settle on their haunches, rest their faces on their paws, and yawn. "You two are unbelievable."

Their tails wagged.

"I didn't mean it as a compliment."

Their tails wagged harder.

I picked up my mug and finished the last of my coffee.

Ding dong.

Max and Finn jumped to their paws and took off running.

I stayed at my desk. Aggie could answer the door.

Brnng, brngg.

I scowled at the phone, even as I cursed whoever was on the other end of the line.

Brnng, brnng.

My scowl deepened.

Brnng, brnng.

"Jones residence." My voice was flat.

"Ellison, is that you?"

I recognized Jinx's voice. "Yes."

"Is it true?" she demanded. She cut straight to the chase.

But which chase? There were so many options. "Is what true?"

"Was Sandy Wilcox arrested for Baxter and Audrey's murders? Someone saw her being put in a squad car at your house. Now the whole town is talking."

Oh. That. "Not true."

"Then why was she taken off in a police car? What did she do?"

Poor Sandy, she'd been so worried about a scandal. "The officer was giving her a ride."

"Sure, he was." Jinx's sarcasm dripped heavy. "Because policemen are helpful like that. Whenever I need a ride, I call a policeman."

"Ha. Ha. Sandy was distraught, and Anarchy didn't want her driving."

"Distraught over what?"

This was what made talking to Jinx so challenging. She asked too many questions, and always the ones I didn't want to answer. "If I tell you, you have to keep it to yourself."

"I promise."

"Anarchy was questioning Grant, and Sandy came to the house to tell me her husband is innocent."

"Wait, Anarchy was questioning Grant about the murders?"

I'd done it again. I needed more coffee (probably an entire urn) before I had this conversation with Jinx.

"Did he kill them?" she asked.

"I have no idea."

"You're sure about that?" First sarcasm, now suspicion.

"I'm sure Anarchy hasn't made an arrest."

She grunted. It was not a happy grunt. "We haven't talked since Emma Tremblay's engagement party."

That was a safer subject "What do you want to know?"

"Donna Miller tackled the poor girl and tried to rip the engagement ring off her finger." It wasn't a question. Jinx knew what had happened. She was looking for confirmation.

"It was horrifying."

"Four karats?"

"Also, true."

"Is Emma going to marry him?"

I didn't want to betray Marilyn's confidence. "Last I heard, yes."

"Young love will forgive anything."

I thought about Sandy Wilcox. "Not just young love."

"What will happen to the house?"

"What do you mean?"

"Morton and Donna can't stay in Kansas City. I supposed Morton could. By all accounts, he's decent looking, and there's plenty of money. True?"

"True."

"If he divorces her, all will be forgiven."

I thought back to the women who'd gathered in Gib's living room. Circling. Eager. Bordering on desperate. Morton would be forgiven. In a heartbeat. I wished the divorcées luck. They'd need it, because I strongly suspected that Honoria would be vetting Morton's next wife.

"Ellison." Aggie stood in the entrance to the den. "I'm sorry to interrupt your call, but Helen Phelps is here to see you."

Ugh. "Jinx, Helen is here. I've got to go. I'll talk to you later." After a gallon of coffee.

We hung up, and I rose from my chair. "Where is she?"

"I put her in the living room."

"Is there any more coffee?"

"I'll start a fresh pot."

"Thank you." With slow steps, I made my way to the living room.

Helen perched on the edge of the sofa. She stood when she

saw me. "Is it true? Have the police arrested the person who killed Baxter?" The grief that had wrapped around her at Gib's was gone. Today, she seemed nervous, edgy as if having Baxter's killer roaming loose was wearing on her.

"I honestly don't know. Aggie is making fresh coffee. May I offer you a cup?"

"Please." She sank back onto the cushion and silently wrung her hands.

"Anarchy will catch Baxter's killer. I promise."

Helen looked up from her lap. "Sandy pretended to be my friend."

"There's no evidence that Sandy killed your husband."

"At least three people called to tell me she was arrested in front of your house."

"She wasn't arrested."

"She was taken off in a police car."

"Yes. But not because she murdered Baxter."

"If it wasn't Sandy, it must have been the mob." She returned her gaze to her hands in her lap. "I don't like to talk about it, but Baxter had a gambling problem."

"Someone may have mentioned that."

"Baxter was given to addictions. Gambling was among the worst of them."

"He had other addictions?"

"The man is dead. I prefer not to air his dirty laundry."

Was there such a thing as a sex addiction? Did Helen know about Club K?

Aggie appeared with a coffee tray and said, "If you don't need anything else, I'll take the dogs for a short walk."

I tilted my head as if a new angle would help access a fresh thought that was just out of reach. "Thank you, Aggie. Oh, look. She's brought us cookies. Aggie's cookies are almost as good as her Bundt cakes." They might be better. Eating a cookie didn't make me feel as guilty as eating a slice of cake. "Do you take cream or sugar?"

"Black."

I poured Helen's coffee and inhaled deeply as the delicious aroma rose from her cup.

Helen put a shortbread on her saucer and shook her head sadly. "I wish I knew what was going on."

"You should ask Anarchy. As Baxter's widow, I'm sure he'll share whatever information he can."

Helen sipped her coffee, as I poured my own cup.

Then I helped myself to a shortbread. "Were Baxter and Grant Wilcox close?"

"Not particularly. Why do you ask?"

Because they shared a sex partner. No way was she getting an honest answer. "Because you and Sandy seem like such good friends."

"We live close by and often walk first thing in the morning."

"The Wilcoxes live in Fairway. You live in Mission Hills."

"We're still only a few blocks away. Most mornings, I walk over to her house. Then we walk to the Shawnee Indian Mission."

I took a bite of my cookie. Sandy with sugar. Buttery. Melt-in-my-mouth good. "That's a good long walk."

She shrugged. "I like walking."

Oh dear Lord. The thought from earlier was back and fully reachable. We'd missed a suspect. An obvious one. "Try the cookie. It really is marvelous."

Helen nibbled, smiling her approval.

"How is Jessica?"

"Jessica will be fine." Her voice was firm. Certain.

"And what about you?"

She finished off her cookie and reached for another. "I'll be fine, too."

I reached out and squeezed her free hand. "Why don't I bring

Anarchy by later today? You can ask him your questions, and he'll tell you whatever he can."

"That's very kind of you."

"I know what it's like to lose a husband to murder."

She winced and stood. "Thank you, Ellison."

I too rose. "Shall we say three o'clock?"

"I'll be expecting you."

I walked her to the front door and watched as she drove away. Then I fetched the coffee tray and dirty cups and returned them to the kitchen. "Aggie?"

She didn't answer, and the dogs weren't underfoot.

Drat. Aggie knew where seldom-used things were kept.

"Do we have a city map?" I asked Mr. Coffee.

I know that look. You've had an epiphany. I knew you'd solve the case. Mr. Coffee was my biggest cheerleader.

"I need a map."

The desk in the study?

"Good idea."

By the time Aggie and the dogs returned, I had the map spread across the kitchen island.

Aggie, whose face was flushed the same soft red as her kaftan, poured herself a glass of water. "What are you doing?"

"Look at this. This is where Baxter's body was found." I pointed to a large green space—the golf course as it appeared on the map. I'd even marked the parking lot's exact location with a red star. "That right there—" I tapped a second red star with my fingernail "—is Audrey Miles' house."

"What about the third star?" Aggie pointed at the map.

"That's the Phelps' home."

"Okay…"

"They're within easy walking distance of each other."

"So?"

"So, Helen Phelps does not have an alibi. She could have walked to Audrey's and killed her."

"But what about her husband?"

"He showed up at Audrey's, and she killed him, too."

"Why move his body?"

"If he was found at Audrey's, it might look like he was killed by a jealous spouse. She shot him, put his body in the trunk of his car, parked it at the club, then walked home." I traced her route on the map. "Her car never left the driveway. And her neighbor, Sherry, remained convinced that Helen was home all night."

"Can you prove it?"

I winced. "We need the gun."

"Is this enough for Anarchy to get a warrant?"

"If he found the right judge? Maybe."

"And if he can't find the right judge?"

"We're going to Helen's this afternoon so that Anarchy can update her on the case."

Aggie's brows rose. "That scenario never works out well for you."

I pretended not to know what she meant. "What scenario?"

"The one where you confront a killer."

"It'll be fine. Anarchy will be there with me."

HELEN WELCOMED ANARCHY AND ME TO HER HOME WITH A tentative smile on her serious face. "Thank you for coming."

"Our pleasure," I replied. I'd shown Anarchy my map and explained my theory. He'd nodded slowly. When I'd told him about our appointment with Helen, he'd tried to talk me out of coming. As if I'd let him go by himself.

"Please." Helen opened the door wider. "Come in out of the heat."

Anarchy stepped inside. I felt a tingle on my neck and glanced over my shoulder. A dark sedan cruised past us.

"Ellison?"

"Sorry. Coming." I crossed the threshold, and Helen closed the door.

We followed her to the living room.

"May I offer you anything to drink?"

"No, thank you," Anarchy replied.

"Ellison?"

"No, thank you."

"Please." She waved toward a pair of chairs covered in faded chintz. "Have a seat." She chose the loveseat across from us, then asked, "What can you tell me about my husband's murder, detective?"

"Your husband and Audrey Miles were killed with the same gun."

I watched Helen's face carefully. She didn't react. Not so much as a blink.

"You don't seem surprised, Mrs. Phelps."

"What? I'm shocked. Very shocked. I can't imagine why anyone would kill Baxter, much less Audrey Miles."

"You weren't aware that your husband had an ongoing relationship with Mrs. Miles?"

"No, I was not." Helen fisted her hands. "And I don't believe it."

"We have corroboration of their affair. The killer went to Audrey Miles' home, murdered her, then your husband. The killer moved your husband's body."

"You can't possibly know that."

"His blood was found at Mrs. Miles' home."

I had no idea if Anarchy was telling the truth, but he sounded convincing. Again, I glanced at Helen. Her cheeks had gone pale.

"Mrs. Miles, not your husband, was the primary target. His murder wasn't a mob hit. You killed him."

Helen recoiled as if he'd slapped her. Her left hand raked through her hair, and her right burrowed in the sofa cushions.

"Anarchy." My voice was a warning. A warning that came too late.

Helen pointed a gun at my chest.

"You should have stayed home." Anarchy had his service revolver aimed at Helen's heart. His eyes were narrowed to slits, and his lips were a thin line.

"Hindsight." I didn't mention that Aggie had foretold this situation. "Tell us why you did it, Helen." There had to be something wrong with me. I wasn't worried about dying. Somehow I knew Anarchy would keep me safe.

"I put up with so much. Years of gambling and lies and robbing Peter to pay Paul. Then, finally, when we'd lost almost everything, he went to rehab. And he got better. We had eleven months of peace. Eleven months before he started disappearing again. I watched our bank accounts like a hawk. But there was never a dime missing. I confronted him, and he swore he was just going to Gamblers Anonymous meetings. But, when you live with an addict, you learn to spot their lies." Her voice shook. Her hand didn't.

If she wasn't aiming a gun at me, if she hadn't killed two people, I might have felt some sympathy for her. I faked it. "That sounds awful."

She nodded. "It was. I even followed him. He was going to some warehouse in the West Bottoms. They wouldn't let me in. I assumed dog fights or boxing or cock fights. It never occurred to me that Baxter was going to a sex club. Not till Grant Wilcox told me about Baxter and Audrey."

Grant Wilcox had a lot to answer for.

"I only went to her house that night to confront her."

"You took a gun." Anarchy's tone was steely.

"She wouldn't listen. And I was so angry…"

"So you shot her."

"I didn't mean to shoot her. It was an accident."

"You shot her in the stomach. It took a while for her to bleed out. You could have called for help."

"She knew how it feels when your husband cheats. She knew. And she took up with Baxter."

"You shot her, you let her bleed to death, and when Baxter showed up, you shot him."

"He wanted to call the police. He insisted. As if he had the moral high ground. Yes, I shot him. He deserved it after everything he put me through."

"You put his body in the trunk of his car and took it to the club. You even doused him with gasoline. Why didn't you light a match?"

"I couldn't do that to Jessica."

"I'm arresting you for the murders of Audrey Miles and Baxter Phelps."

"No. You're not." Her gun was still aimed at my chest. "Ellison and I are going to take a little drive. If you follow me, I'll kill her. If you let me go, I'll release her at the first rest stop out of town."

Oh dear Lord. Why? Why did these things keep happening to me?

Helen jerked her head toward the foyer. "Move."

I looked to Anarchy for guidance.

His expression was thunderous. "Go with her."

Slowly, I bent and picked up my handbag.

Helen shook her head. "You don't need that."

"You're planning on stranding me at a rest stop. I most certainly do." I also needed the gun I'd tucked inside.

Helen tossed me a set of keys. "You're driving."

When we reached the foyer, Helen told Anarchy to open the front door. "You exit first. Ellison and I will follow. If you try anything, I'll shoot her." Either she'd given this a great deal of thought, or she'd watched too many cop shows.

We stepped outside into the bright sunshine and a loud bang had me falling to the grass. Panic consumed me. Was Anarchy injured?

Squealing tires drew my focus, and I watched a dark sedan speed away.

"Anarchy?" For the first time this afternoon, I felt actual fear. Had Frank shot him?

"Ellison, are you hurt?" My husband crouched next to Helen. She was bleeding. A lot.

"How badly is she hurt?"

"Right shoulder. She'll be fine." He stood and kicked her gun out of reach. "Can you call this in?"

"Of course."

"Ellison." His voice stopped me at the door. "The shooter?"

"Frank."

"I figured. I owe him one."

CHAPTER TWENTY-TWO

The American Restaurant had a fabulous view of the downtown skyline. It was also a gorgeous space. Bentwood pillars opened into delicate fans on the ceiling. The booths were decadently comfortable. And, of course, the food was divine.

"Sis arrives tomorrow?" Honoria sat next to me with a glass of Champagne held firmly in her hand.

"Tomorrow morning. The nine o'clock flight."

"And she's bringing your children."

"She is." I couldn't help but smile. I'd missed them terribly.

She tilted the rim of her glass toward me. "To satisfactory resolutions."

"No matter what it takes to achieve them?" I eyed the scratch marks on the back of Emma's left hand until the light caught her ring and nearly blinded me.

"One can't make an omelet without breaking a few eggs." Honoria was a terrifying woman. "Tell me about this woman who killed her husband."

"She confessed. She'll be in prison for a long time." I sipped my seltzer and lime.

"You were there."

"I was."

Honoria leveled her beady gaze on me. "Emma tells me that Fairway is a nice neighborhood. I'm surprised there was a drive-by shooting."

Anarchy, who sat across the table from me, cleared his throat. "It was a one-in-a-million coincidence."

"A sedan drove by, and someone in it just happened to shoot the woman pointing a gun at your wife? I should say so."

I shrugged. "I got lucky."

Her lips quirked. "A satisfactory resolution?"

"Let's call it that." I leaned closer to her. "Where is Donna?"

"She ran back to Boston to hire a divorce lawyer. Not that it will do her any good. She signed a pre-nup when she married Morton."

We both shifted our gazes to Emma and Price, and Honoria's expression softened. "I'm glad Emma wasn't too traumatized."

"She's loves him."

She patted my hand. "My family isn't usually so dramatic."

"Really? Mine is."

MEET POPPY FIELDS

Poppy Fields, Hollywood influencer extraordinaire, just agreed to a week at the newest, most luxurious resort in Cabo. After all, what's better than the beach when a girl is feeling blue?

When Poppy is abducted, she'll need all her smarts, all her charm, and a killer Chihuahua, to save herself.

Dead body #1 found in bed, with me. That was a shock.

Dead body #2 found in bed, not with me. That was a relief.

Dead body #3 died telling me I'm a lousy actress. I already knew that.

Dead body #4 died trying to kill me.

Dead body #5 died kidnapping me.

Dead body #6 died guarding me.

Dead body #7 was a really bad man.

Dead body #8 was an even worse man.

That's a lot of dead bodies for a girl looking for a week's relaxation in Cabo. And, I'm probably leaving a few out--math isn't my thing. Unless I can escape the cartel, I'll be #9.

CHAPTER 1

I f Chariss said it once, she said it a thousand times. "It's a good thing you don't want to be an actress. The only thing you're fit for is screwball comedies and they're dead."

Those words ran through my head.

Not the actress part. I didn't want to be an actress. That whole dive into real emotions and share them with the world thing? No, thank you.

But the screwball comedy part? Chariss had a point. My life was a screwball comedy.

How else to explain my current dilemma?

I was naked and locked in a bathroom. A man I'd sworn never to speak to again slept on the other side of the door.

I closed my eyes and saw myself as Kate Hudson which would make him Matthew McConaughey. He'd like the sexy part of that comparison. Even with my eyes closed I saw his slow grin—felt his slow grin. All the way to my toes.

Nope. Never again.

Never.

Today was the start of a new life.

No more drinking. No more clubs. No more sexy, dangerous men who were bad for me.

Especially not the one in the bedroom.

I crossed my heart, hoped to die (that might actually be happening—my head hurt that badly), and rested my forehead against the locked door.

What did I drink last night? I had vague recollections of a bar. Dark pulsing lights. Dark pulsing music. Test tubes filled with something sweet. The man.

The ridiculously sexy man.

Jake.

How many times could one woman make the same mistake? Apparently, a zillion.

Or at least three.

Why hadn't I grabbed my phone before my mad dash to the bathroom?

Screwball comedy. It was the only answer.

I lurched (Frankenstein, but less graceful) to the sink, turned on the tap, and drank deeply. Straight from the faucet. My mouth wasn't just dry. Dry would have felt like a spring shower compared to the arid wasteland behind my gums. I drank till my stomach sloshed then I ran my tongue over my teeth.

Moss.

Where the hell was the toothpaste? Not on the counter. Not in any obvious place. I rubbed a wet finger against my teeth. Better than nothing. Slightly. Then I held a hand in front of my mouth, exhaled, and sniffed.

Ugh. If I wanted to get rid of Jake forever, all I had to do was breathe on him. How was it even possible for breath to smell that bad?

I needed toothpaste and something—anything—for my headache.

Where?

The whole damned bathroom was white marble and mirrors

(I would not look in those mirrors—would not). No drawers. No medicine cabinets. No razor or hairbrush or deodorant. No Ambien or Xanax or even Excedrin. Just white marble and a single bar of soap.

I splashed water around my eyes, reached for the soap, and sniffed. Jo Malone. Jake's favorite.

The man hadn't brought a toothbrush but he remembered his precious soap.

The scents of lime, basil and mandarin did nothing for the roiling in my stomach but I washed my hands and face. After I rinsed, the scents—his scents—lingered.

The towel I used was über-fluffy. Hotel fluffy.

A hotel?

Please, no. I squeezed my eyes closed and broke out in a tequila-scented sweat.

A walk of shame through a hotel lobby was more than I could bear. And if anyone took a picture… I rested my palms on the edge of the counter, opened my eyes, and faced the woman in the mirror.

A celery-hued paleness in my cheeks spoke of a wild night. That and the bags beneath my bloodshot eyes. I could pack for Europe in those bags. And my hair? I poked at it. Gingerly. As if my finger might get stuck. I'd crossed a screwball comedy line —Kate Hudson would never look this awful.

God help me if there were photographers in the lobby.

I wrapped myself in a towel, staggered to the door, and pressed my ear against its cool expanse.

Not a peep on the other side.

I cracked the door.

Thank God the room wasn't bright. As it was, I squinted into the lavender glow of early morning sneaking through the gaps in the drapes. The dim light revealed a dresser littered with glasses and a half-empty tequila bottle.

There. Panties on the floor. Bra, black against the bed's white sheets. Dress, draped across the chair. Shoes? I'd find them when I wasn't naked.

I tiptoed toward the panties. Tiptoed, because talking to the man in the bed might be the only thing worse than my headache.

He didn't move. Not an inch.

I hooked the panties with my big toe (bending over wasn't an option—my brains might leak out of my ears), kicked them into the air, caught them and, using the bedpost for balance, slid them on.

With one hand still clutching the towel, I tiptoed to my side of the bed and reached for the bra tangled among the pillows. I tugged. And tugged. Dammit. I tugged harder and the wisp of silk and lace came free. I stumbled backward—thunk—right into the bedside table.

A glass teetering on the table's edge fell onto the hardwood floor and shattered.

The crash reverberated through the bedroom—through my skull. Loud. So loud. Loud enough to wake the dead. I didn't breathe. I didn't move.

Jake slept.

The tequila bottle on the dresser snickered and wagged a judgmental finger at me. You're so clumsy when you're hung over.

I narrowed my eyes and shot Señor Cuervo a death glare. Who was I kidding with the Señor? José and I were on a first-name basis. Go to hell, José.

What would I say if Jake did wake up? About last night, remember when I said never again? I totally meant it. Now. This moment. This morning. Us. It's a mistake. It won't happen again. Ever. He'd just smile that cat-and-canary smile of his and charm me back into bed.

Why? Why, why, why?

I knew better.

He knew better.

But my life was a screwball comedy so, of course, I'd gone to bed with the man who'd broken my heart. Twice.

I stood straighter. I was over him. Getting over him had taken more tears, bottles of tequila, and quarts of ice cream than I cared to count. But he'd been out of my system. And now this.

If I snuck out without talking to him, my heart might not shatter.

All I needed was my dress.

A sea of broken glass separated me from the black silk. If I'd felt halfway decent, I could have leapt over the shards.

I didn't feel an eighth of the way decent. Every muscle in my body hurt. What exactly had we done to make my calves ache?

Never mind—lalalalalala—I didn't want to know.

If I stepped there and there and there, I could reach the dress without shredding my feet.

One step. Two steps. Thre—

"Son of a bi—" I clamped one hand over my mouth and hopped on my uninjured foot. Hop. Hop. Hop. Into the dresser.

Thunk.

Pain shot through my hip.

That would leave a mark.

The tequila bottle snickered again.

Well. José and I were done. Forever. I meant it this time (unlike those other times—those other times were passing fancies). I shot him another death glare. Done. Adios. Finito. Don't let the door hit you on the way out.

José smirked.

I planned my route to the damned dress. Just a few steps. Easy steps without a cut foot and an epic hangover. With both...

I had this.

Step.

Step.

One. More. Step.

I leaned. I reached. I snatched the dress off the chair.

Jake didn't move. Thank God for small favors.

I shimmied into my dress. Shoes? Where were they?

I looked down at my feet. A pool of blood had formed beneath my toes.

No way was I jamming a bloody foot into my new Louboutins. Maybe there was a bandage in that bathroom. At least there was a towel. I limped back to all that whiteness leaving a bloody trail behind me.

The bathroom really was enormous. The glass shower enclosure was larger than most cars and the damned mirrors went on for miles. And there were towels. Lots of them. They batted their eyelashes at me—a come-hither invitation. God, I wanted a shower.

As soon as I got home, I'd stand under a piping hot stream of water until last night's sins (even the forgotten ones) were washed away.

I crouched and poked on the flat surface of the cabinet below the sink until a door popped open. Inside, I found yet another stack of towels, washcloths, and an industrial size bottle of aspirin. Nothing else.

First things first.

Aspirin. I forged a long and valiant battle with the child-proof lid.

Victory!

I swallowed three pills, washing them down with more water from the tap. Then I grabbed a washcloth, sat on the toilet, and pressed the cloth against my foot.

It felt good to sit. Spend-the-day-there good.

If only he weren't in the bedroom, liable to wake up at any time.

I pulled the cloth away from my foot and eyed the cut. A shard of glass glinted in the morning light.

Hell.

I gritted my teeth and pulled the sliver out of my skin. More blood. An ocean of blood. I should-have-grabbed-two-washcloths blood.

I pressed the crimson-soaked cloth against the cut. Pressure. That was the ticket.

And another washcloth. That was the other ticket.

I limped back to the sink, grabbed two additional cloths, and held them against my foot until the bleeding stopped.

Then I returned to the bedroom.

The light had shifted from lavender to lemon. And, God bless him, Jake still slept.

I spotted my handbag (a black clutch just big enough for my cell, I.D., and credit card) on the dresser next to the tequila. Where were the shoes? I wasn't leaving without them.

There. One near the foot of the bed, the other on the floor near his head.

I tiptoed to the shoe at the bottom of the bed, snagged the sandal, and hung it around my wrist from its strap. Then I crept toward the remaining shoe.

Got it!

Jake still hadn't moved. At all.

He was so deeply asleep I could brush one last kiss across his lips before I disappeared. He'd never know.

Stupid? Totally. What if he woke up?

But what if I walked away without kissing him one last time? A kiss I'd actually remember.

My eyes filled with tears. I blamed the tequila-induced headache.

I inched back the duvet.

Jake's head rested on a pillow and I took a few seconds to memorize his face in repose. He was handsome in a chiseled Hollywood movie-star way. His only visible flaw, a small crescent-shaped scar on his chin. The invisible flaws were many. I rubbed my eyes. I would not cry. Would not. My eyes were blood-shot enough already.

He was more trouble than he was worth.

He was too good looking.

He was not my type. (Liar, liar.)

He'd broken my heart. Twice.

I leaned down and brushed a last kiss against his cheek. There. Done. No reason to stay. But I paused.

His cheek was clammy.

"Are you sick?" My voice was hardly louder than the hum of the air conditioner.

He didn't move.

Of course he didn't. He'd slept through my shattering crystal and hopping around the bedroom like a demented kangaroo. A little thing like a whisper would hardly wake him.

The smart thing would be to sneak out. Disappear.

But what if he needed help?

I rested my hand against his forehead.

His skin was damp and waxy.

What was wrong with his mouth? Was that foam?

"Jake!"

He didn't move. Not an inch.

I poked him. "Jake!"

Nothing.

Oh my God. Oh. My. God.

I stumbled backward. My heart thudded against my chest. My lungs refused to take in air.

I collapsed into an armchair and pressed the heels of my palms against my eye sockets. One of my sandals scratched at my neck. I threw the stilettos onto the floor. Their red soles looked like blood.

With shaking fingers, I reached for the phone on the bedside table and dialed 9-1-1.

"What's your emergency?" The operator's voice was cool and professional.

"I need an ambulance."

"What's your emergency, ma'am?"

"It's my boyfr—it's my—he's cold and clammy and he's not moving."

"Is he breathing?" asked the voice.

"I can't tell—" my voice caught "—I think he might have overdosed."

"Do you know his name, ma'am?"

"Of course." Heat rose from my chest to my cheeks. I wasn't that girl—the girl who woke up with questionable men. Except, this morning, I was. "His name is Jake Smith."

A few seconds ticked by. Seconds I spent staring at Jake's pale face.

"Are you there, ma'am?"

"Yes." Talking required effort, and between the pain in my head and the pain in my heart, I was fresh out of effort.

"Where are you?"

I looked around the bedroom for clues. There were none. "I don't know." How pathetic was that?

"Are you safe?" the operator asked.

"Yes."

"What's your name?"

I could lie. I considered it. But my blood and fingerprints were everywhere. The police would find me. "Poppy Fields."

There it was—the pause of recognition. When your mother was one of the biggest stars in Hollywood, people knew your name. "I'm tracing the landline now, Ms. Fields. Help is on the way. Can you tell me what happened?" The operator was trained to keep me talking. I knew that. I'd seen it on one of those true crime shows.

"I woke up and he was like this." Beyond that, everything—

the previous night, how we'd come to this place, what we'd done
—was lost in a dense fog.

The tequila bottle shook its self-righteous head. No one made
you drink me.

"Officers will arrive in approximately two minutes. Can you
let them in?"

"Yes." I hauled myself out of the chair. My head objected.
Strongly. How was it possible to hurt this much?

"Stay on the line with me, Ms. Fields."

"I'll be fine. Thank you for your help." I put the receiver
back in its cradle and crossed the bedroom. The door opened
onto a hallway filled with light. Wincing at the brightness,
I made my way to the stairs. My hand closed around the bannister—clutched around the bannister. A wave of dizziness swept
through me. I would not throw up. Would not.

The police were coming. I had to open the door.

Except the door at the bottom of the stairs already stood ajar,
allowing a slice of sunlight to cut across the floor, sharp as the
pieces of the broken crystal on the bedroom floor.

I collapsed onto the bottom step and looked around. I knew
where I was—Jake's friend's house. I rested my throbbing head
in my hands. Jake would be all right. He had to be. Our story
couldn't end this way. Jake being dead wasn't part of a screwball
comedy. Jake being dead was tragic.

"Ma'am?"

I lifted my head.

A police officer in a dark blue uniform stared at me. "Are
you all right, ma'am?" His concern sounded genuine.

"Jake's upstairs." I gripped the bannister and pulled myself to
standing. "This way."

A second police officer entered the foyer. This one regarded
me with narrowed eyes, his gaze traveling from my bare feet to the
barely-there length of my dress. The corner of his upper lip curled.

I read his nametag. Officer Crane.

How dare he pass judgment? It wasn't like I was a ditsy party girl who drank too much and spent the night with men I shouldn't. Well, not usually. And it wasn't like Jake was a one-night stand. He was an ex I'd hooked up with. Maybe. Why couldn't I remember?

"This way." I led the police officers up the stairs to the master bedroom. "In there."

They pushed past me, surveyed the bedroom (tangled sheets, broken crystal, and bloodied floor), and approached the bed. "Sir?"

"Is he all right?" He wasn't. But pretending felt better than the truth.

Officer Crane ignored me. "Sir?"

Jake didn't answer.

The police officer poked Jake in the shoulder and got no response (I could have told him poking wouldn't work). Then Officer Crane turned on the bedside lamp and took a good look at the man in the bed. The color leached out of Officer Crane's face.

What? What was wrong? I stepped inside the bedroom.

The police officers didn't seem to notice me. Their gazes were fixed on the man in the bed.

Officer Crane looked up, spearing me with a glare. "What kind of drugs did you take?"

I shook my head. "I didn't take any drugs."

"What kind did he take?" His lip curled until it kissed his nose.

"He didn't." That I knew of. "He didn't."

He snorted. "We'll see what an autopsy says about that."

CHAPTER 2

The sun setting over the Pacific gilded the sky and limned wisps of clouds in shades of crimson and bronze. The glorious colors reflected on the plane's wing. Breathtaking. It was the kind of sunset people from fly-over states paid good money to see.

I swallowed a yawn and shifted my gaze from the fading sun to the brightest star in Hollywood.

His disapproving gaze was settled firmly upon me. "Are you going to this resort opening because they're paying you?"

"Yes." The lie was a small one and easier than explaining my need to escape.

He pursed his lips. "If you're hard up for money all you need to do is ask." Then James Ballester offered me the smile that had melted a million women's hearts. "You know that, right? Anything I have is yours." James and my mother made four movies together. Each one grossed more than five-hundred-million dollars. Anything covered a lot of ground.

"You should be careful. Someday I may take you up on that."

He reached across the space that separated us and took my

hand. His fingers were warm and dry and elegant. His gaze shifted from my face to the last rays of sunshine glinting off the plane's wing, then he reached deep within himself and found his soulful expression. If his smile didn't melt a woman's heart, the soulful expression would. Guaranteed. And once her heart was melted, she'd fall in line with his plans.

Even I blinked. And I knew the soulful expression was an act. A face practiced in front of a mirror until it was perfect.

His grip on my hand tightened. "I mean it, Poppy. What's going on with you? If you need money, tell me."

"I'm fine." And I was—at least when it came to money. I wasn't mega-movie-star-rich but I wasn't scrounging for my next meal—or even my next first-class plane ticket. "I hate flying commercial and when Chariss said you were going to Mexico—"

"Honey, you can use my plane anytime. I don't have to be on it." That soulful expression of his—it said he adored me, would do anything for me, would even give me an airplane and its crew.

There were three things the movie-ticket-buying public didn't know about James Ballester. One—he was genuinely nice. Two—he was incredibly generous. Three—he was gay.

America's heartthrob preferred men.

For all the talk about acceptance and rainbows and inclusion, women still wanted the man they were lusting after to lust after them. James was so deeply in the closet, he had one foot in Narnia.

He amped up the soulful look. His eyes shone. His lips parted. He looked as if he was about to offer to walk through hell and back for me. "Tell me why you're going to this resort."

"I'm doing a favor for a friend."

He raised a brow and tilted his head, a silent demand for a better answer.

I didn't have a better answer. "André promised them A-listers." Not a lie but not the truth. Telling the truth might break me.

Lying to James—I squeezed his hand—was wrong. When my dad disappeared, and I moved in with Chariss, it was James who acted like a parent. Not Chariss. Chariss never wanted to be a mother. Not when I was a baby. Certainly not when I was a teenager with an attitude. For nearly ten years, James, not the woman who'd given birth to me, had been the closest thing I had to family.

"André DuChamp?" James' lips thinned and the space between his eyes scrunched together—as if even the mention of André's name was distasteful.

James judged André based on his father's sins. And an epic flop was as big a sin as there was in Hollywood.

"Yes, André DuChamp."

James released my hand and crossed his arms over his chest. "Let me guess—the DuChamp kid didn't get any A-listers, so he needed you."

The DuChamp kid? Really? André was a huge success. He hadn't reached his quota of A-listers. He'd surpassed it. My friend was the agent to the temporarily famous. Housewives (both desperate and blogging), rejected bachelorettes, and Kardashian wanna-bes—they all wanted André representing them. And when they posted on Instagram about juice cleanses or charcoal tooth powder or their fabulous vacations, André made a cut.

Reality stars who auctioned off their fifteen minutes of fame on Instagram were one of James' pet peeves. André was another. "How much is this resort paying you? How often do you have to post?"

"It's not like that." The thought of escaping to Cabo had been so tempting—an escape from grief and guilt and loneliness—and all I had to do was pose for a few pictures at the opening night party. Thirty minutes of my time, and the resort would give me a luxury villa for the week. "Like I said, this is a favor."

"Forget about the resort. Come to La Paz with me. At the end of the week, I'll fly you to Paris."

Paris. Chariss was shooting a movie in Paris and I was supposed to visit the set. "What's this film about?" After a while, the films and the parts ran together.

"Chariss is playing a woman who pits herself against a drug cartel after the man she loves dies."

I laughed—a guffaw tied around a sob.

James' expression turned disapproving. "It's not a comedy."

I shook my head—the only apology I could manage without falling apart.

He tilted his head and the slight wrinkle between his brows deepened. "Do you think she's too old for the part?"

"Of course not." I spoke quickly. Decisively. Glad to talk about Chariss. Glad to discuss my mother's age rather than Jake.

Chariss and my dad met when she was eighteen and married in a summer-long fit of lust. I arrived nine months later. I wasn't a month old when a television pilot Chariss made before my parents met got picked up. Chariss was gone. It was Dad and me for fourteen years. When he disappeared, Chariss, who'd been passing for a woman in her twenties, had to explain how she had a teenage daughter. Making such an explanation hadn't made her happy. Nor did my current age of twenty-three. Neither math nor advancing years were Chariss's friends.

"Forty is the new twenty." I was willing to fudge math facts on her behalf. "She's still the most beautiful woman in the world." Why was I arguing her case? Any number of magazines had already decided that, despite middle age creeping up behind her, Chariss Carlton was more fabulous than ever. They trumpeted her ageless beauty on their covers. Scribed articles about being sexy and forty. Chariss didn't need me—didn't want me—standing up for her.

"When you wrinkle your nose like that, you look just like her." James meant well. He did. But being a carbon copy of Chariss Carlton wasn't the bed of roses everyone imagined.

I wiped away the expression.

James settled back into the buttery soft leather of his seat. "There's something bothering you. I can tell. Level with me."

"I'm fine."

"You shouldn't go alone."

"I'm not. Mia is coming." Another lie. Mia, my best friend, was the daughter of a country-star who'd defined a decade.

James' gaze settled on the empty seat next to me.

"Mia takes two days to pack a gym bag. There's no way she could have made this flight. She'll get in tomorrow." What was one more lie in the greater scheme of things?

"I've got a bad feeling about this."

"I'll be fine. It's a five-star resort. What could happen?"

"You could be kidnapped."

"I won't leave the grounds. I promise."

"You could get food poisoning." Now he was clutching at straws.

"I sincerely doubt that."

"You could—" he shifted his gaze to the darkening sky "—you could need someone and you'll be alone."

Lately, that was nothing new. "I'll be fine."

James pursed his lips. "Mexico can be a dangerous place. So much violence. Did you see the news stories about the grain alcohol some of the resorts served? We won't even talk about the drugs."

Drugs. An open sesame word.

The police detective investigating Jake's death, Detective Parks, houdinied his way out of the locked steamer trunk in my brain and took the seat next to me. He crossed his left ankle over his right knee. He laced his fingers behind his neck. He leaned back in his seat. And he leveled his suspicious gaze right at me.

I ground my teeth.

"What's wrong?" asked James.

"Nothing." I focused on James and ignored not-really-there Detective Parks and his accusatory gaze.

"You don't look fine."

I forced a smile. "I'm on my way to a week of luxury relaxation." I couldn't afford to scowl at the phantom sitting next to me.

"Why didn't you bring that man you've been seeing?"

My heart lurched and my smile faded.

"Did you break up?" James softened. He was ready with sympathy or anger—depending on my answer.

The one thing—the one person—I didn't want to talk about. I shook my head, unable to speak. I'd be okay if I could keep the grief and guilt locked inside.

"Poppy." James' brow furrowed. His eyes questioned. "Tell me what happened."

I couldn't keep lying. Not to James. I swallowed the enormous lump in my throat. "He died." My voice was small.

"Died?" James leaned forward in his seat and reclaimed my hands. His face was a mask of concern. "What happened?"

My throat tightened and I tilted my head and stared at the ceiling of the plane. "He overdosed."

"Oh, honey." His grip on my hands tightened.

Guilt, tired of idly nibbling, sank its sharp teeth deep into my psyche and shook me like a ragdoll. It had been doing that a lot lately.

I'd slept while Jake's life dribbled away.

Infuriating Jake, with his golden hair and golden smile and devilish sense of humor, was gone. If I'd awakened an hour earlier, he might still be alive.

I freed one of my hands from James' grip and patted beneath my eyes.

"When did this happen?"

"A month ago."

"A month? And you're just now telling me?"

"I couldn't." My voice gave out and I gasped for air.

"You can't be alone." James never went anywhere alone. There was always a personal assistant or manager or agent around. Or me.

"I want to be alone." I snuck a peek at Detective Parks. For a figment of my imagination, he was awfully solid. His face was stony—judging me, my lifestyle, my values. At least he remained silent.

The words he'd said when he brought me in for questioning had scored deep wounds. Words like accessory to a homicide and manslaughter—as if I had actively taken part in Jake's death.

"Jake didn't take drugs," I'd insisted.

"Oh?" Detective Parks had packed more disdain in that single syllable than I would have dreamed possible.

"He didn't. Just party drugs." Jake didn't touch anything that could hurt him—not heroin, not meth, not opioids.

"So party drugs aren't real drugs?"

"No." So sure I was right.

"Party drugs are real drugs." Detective Parks had smacked his palm down on the table.

"Oh." A barely there oh.

He glared at me with eyes the color and temperature of ice chips. "There's a synthetic party drug trickling across the border that's five times more deadly than heroin."

"Oh." It was the only thing I could think to say.

"It's probably what killed your boyfriend."

Now I had no words. Not even oh. I'd simply stared at the top of the scarred table and let my tears fall.

"They're calling it Venti."

I glanced up at him. "Venti?"

His mouth twisted. "As if it's a harmless coffee."

"Oh."

"You could make a difference. Stop another death."

"How?"

"Where did he get the stuff?"

I didn't do drugs. Never. Not even Molly. Everyone had heard me say it so often, they'd given up offering me anything. I couldn't help the detective. I didn't know anything. I shook my head.

Detective Parks responded with an I-don't-believe-you scowl.

I'd gone home and cried—ugly cried—till my eyes were swollen and my skin was blotchy. I'd cried till the walls closed in then I'd walked on the beach.

I walked until my tears were spent, until my leg muscles shook with tiny tremors, until sadness nearly swallowed me whole.

Tears, walks on the beach, pints of mint chocolate chip ice cream, and fifths of tequila became my life. Day after day. Grief wouldn't let me go.

When André called and offered me this trip, I'd said yes. Immediately. Cabo. A place where Jake's memory might not haunt me.

"Poppy, you okay? You seem a million miles away." James stood, shifted, and sat next to me (on Detective Parks, who gave me one last this-is-all-your-fault glare before he dissipated).

I found a brave smile (James wasn't the only one who practiced expressions in front of the mirror) and offered it up. "I will be. A week away is just what I need."

His lips parted as if he meant to argue but he wrapped an arm around my shoulders. "Remember, I'm just a phone call away."

James' assistant appeared in the doorway and cleared her throat. "The pilot asked me to tell you we'll be landing in about thirty minutes."

"Thank you." James tightened his hold on me. "I can spend the night if you want."

"Don't you start shooting in the morning?" The producer would have kittens if James showed up a day late.

James pressed my cheek against his chest and stroked my hair. "You're more important than a movie."

That had never been Chariss's philosophy. I leaned into his warmth. "It's a luxury resort. What could go wrong?"

CHAPTER 3

The resort's pool deck was spectacular. Tiered infinity pools spilled down the hillside toward the beach. The water in the pools matched the turquoise of the ocean.

I descended the stairs, pausing on each level until I reached the level with a bar. I approached the bartender. "A bottle of Perrier, please."

His eyes widened slightly. Even here at the tip of Baja, Chariss's face was still recognizable.

He handed me the bottle and I signed a room chit.

Then I made my way to the pool closest to the beach.

A row of chaise lounges topped with bleached linen cushions and carefully folded beach towels the color of a January sky faced the pool and the waves below.

I picked a chaise and unpacked my pool bag. Sunscreen, earbuds, and a novel. What more could I need?

It was only when I was hidden behind the cover of my book that I looked around.

Down the length of the pool deck, a large group celebrated the arrival of morning with tequila shots. Men with bellies or mustaches or large tattoos (or a combination of all three) were surrounded by beautiful women who hung on their every word. Their laughter and the clink of their glasses competed with the sounds of the waves.

I nodded once at a man (no belly, no mustache, no visible tattoo) who stared at me with a speculative tilt to his head. Not happening, buddy. I plugged the earbuds into my cell and drowned the group's noise out with Lorde.

The sun was warm—not too hot. The cushion was comfortable. I put down my book, closed my eyes, and let my mind wander.

It wandered right back to Jake. To the night we met.

He'd sent a drink.

I'd sent it back.

For most men, that rejection would have been enough. Not for Jake. I'd made myself a challenge.

He sauntered over to the table I shared with Mia, offered me a vague nod, then directed his sun-god smile at my friend. "I'm Jake."

The hit-on-her-friend ploy. Been there. Done that. Boring the first time.

I looked at Mia, "You ready?"

Mia dismissed Jake with a flick of her lashes. "Yeah."

We left him at the table and went outside where Donny, Mia's father's driver, waited at the curb in a Bentley.

Donny opened the door and we climbed inside.

"That guy was hot. You're sure you don't want to grab him for the night?"

"Please," I huffed. One-nighters weren't my thing.

"Do you want to go home?"

I shrugged and made a sound that could have been yes or no.

"I'd like to swing by Terra." One of the guys pursuing her was an investor in the club. Whenever she sensed he might be losing interest, she showed up.

"Fine." I made going to the hottest club in L.A. sound like an imposition. "But if you decide to stay, can Donny run me home?"

Talk about impositions. The sudden stiffness in Donny's shoulders and the audible sigh from the front seat said the prospect of a drive to Malibu didn't fill him with joy.

Either Mia didn't notice or she didn't care. "Of course."

Terra was packed, but Thor (I kid you not) led us straight to a table in the VIP section.

We sat.

Mia looked around, tapped her fingers against the table, squirmed in her chair, and stood. "Back in five."

Yeah, right.

One glass of Champagne and I was out of there.

"If I didn't know better, I'd say you were avoiding me."

I looked up and there he was, offering me another sun-god smile.

"How did you get in here?" The VIP section at Terra wasn't easy to crash.

"I know people."

"A couple of guys named Benjamin?"

He had the good grace to flush.

"You know, this borders on stalker-ish."

"Me?" He sounded deeply offended. "Stalker-ish?" Then he broke into song. Stay with Me. And he sounded exactly like Sam Smith. Exactly.

When he sang the last note, there were fifteen women with their tongues hanging out of their mouths. I wasn't one of them.

"Pick from your new fan club."

His eyes sparkled and he gave the sun-god smile another try. He was—dazzling. "Not interested?"

"Neither am I."

He held his hands over his heart as I'd somehow wounded him. "I serenaded you."

"Nice trick. Does it work often?"

"Never fails." He did have a nice smile.

"I'm not a groupie."

"What if I told you I was the lead singer in a high school band?"

"High school bands don't impress me."

There was that smile again. He pulled out Mia's chair.

"And I'm still not interested."

"I'm—"

I waggled my fingers at him. "I'm. Not. Interested."

"One drink? Please?" There was something in the way he said please—as if having a drink with me mattered. "One drink then, if you're still not interested, I'll leave you alone."

He had sounded like Sam Smith. "One drink."

Three tequinis later, I had Donny drive me to the house in Malibu. Alone.

Jake and I met for coffee the next morning.

We met for dinner that night.

He took me sailing.

I took him shopping.

We went to movies. And plays. And concerts.

He spent the night at my place.

I spent the night at his.

He brought over a razor and toothbrush.

I took over a bottle of conditioner and a WaterPik.

He stood me up.

We argued.

He disappeared for a week.

I worried, then I listened to excuses, then I broke things off.

He begged for forgiveness.

I forgave him.

He disappeared again.

I worried, then I listened to excuses, then I broke things off.

He begged for forgiveness.

I didn't forgive him.

Our story wasn't even original. Not until the morning I woke up and he didn't.

"You are too lovely to look so sad." A shadow pulled me from my memories.

For one joyous second, I imagined it was Jake blocking my sun and my heart leapt. Then I remembered Jake was dead and my heart slammed back into my chest.

How could I have made such a mistake? The man in front of me was tall enough, but he was dark. Jake had been golden and sun-kissed. Their auras were different.

Despite the warmth of the sun I shivered.

The tall stranger from down the length of the pool (the one with no belly, no mustache, and no tattoos) stared down at me. "I hope we're not disturbing you." He waved at the group at the opposite end of the pool deck.

Not till now. "Not at all."

"I am Javier."

"Nice to meet you." I lowered my sunglasses and looked up at him. "Poppy."

"Poppy?" His lips flirted with a smile.

My lips did zero flirting. "Mhmm."

"An unusual name."

"Is it?"

He nodded. A definitive nod—as if he was accustomed to having the final say. "You look like an American movie star." Javier wasn't exactly charting new territory. I'd heard a variation of that line one-hundred-forty-three times in the past month.

"Oh?" It was coming. I waited.

"Chariss Carlton." His lips stopped flirting with a smile and actually curved.

I returned my gaze to my book.

"You've heard of her?"

"My mother."

"No!"

"Yes." Here they came—the laundry list of movies including his favorites and the invasive questions. I checked my page number and prepared a yawn.

"Is she here with you?" Not one of the questions I'd been expecting.

I looked up from page fifty-six. "Chariss is shooting a movie in Paris."

"You are here alone?" He stepped closer—too close.

I pressed my back against the cushion and tightened my grip on the book.

An explosion of laughter had us both turning our gazes toward his friends.

One of the men (complete with belly, mustache, and tattoos —the trifecta—plus an ugly scar across his chest) had pulled off one of the women's bikini tops. He held it just out of her reach.

Granted, her reach wasn't far—not with her arms crossed over her chest.

Her gaze traveled from her missing top to Javier and me. She glared at us as if we were somehow to blame.

Whoever she was, she could give Chariss a run for the most-beautiful-woman-in-the-world title. Dark hair floated down her back, her face was a perfect oval, and her skin looked like bronze velvet.

With an explosive guffaw, the man with her top tossed the bits of fabric and string into the pool.

The woman turned her gaze to the water then stood. She stalked to the edge of the pool and dove in. A perfect, elegant dive.

A moment later she emerged from the water fully covered. Droplets from her body showered the pool deck as she made her way to the man with the belly and the mustache and the tattoos and the ugly scar.

She spoke. Softly. I didn't hear her actual words but the

laughter and the smiles on the faces of the people around her disappeared. Wiped away as if they had never been.

The man who'd swiped her top flushed a deep red.

She walked toward Javier and me with her head held high and her shoulders straight.

Her eyes narrowed as she neared us—eyes the exact shade of honey amber.

Javier held up a hand but she brushed past him as if he wasn't there.

He watched her walk away. "Marta."

Her step hitched—barely—but she didn't stop.

I had enough drama without borrowing theirs. I raised my book.

By the time he shifted his gaze back to me, my eyes were glued to page fifty-six. Please, just walk away. Please.

"Perhaps you'd like to join—"

My phone rang. Gypsy from Fleetwood Mac.

Thank God.

"I'm sorry. A friend is calling." Mia had a serious girl-crush on Stevie Nicks—thus the ringtone. I held the phone to my ear. "Hello."

"Where are you?" One day, Mia and her you-are-so-busted tone would strike fear in her children's hearts. Already I felt guilty, and I hadn't done anything.

"I'm in Cabo." And Javier was listening,

"So I hear. James called and wanted to know when my flight was leaving. He's worried about you being alone."

"I want to be alone." Hint, hint, Javier.

"Are you sure? I could fly down there."

"Positive. I just need time." I glanced at Javier. "Alone."

"I know. But why Mexico?"

"Why not?"

"Because, usually when you have a problem, you go to the ranch." Mia knew me too well. "Plus it's dangerous."

"Not at the resorts." I glanced up at Javier, who'd made no move to leave. Obviously, the man couldn't take a hint. I conjured up an apologetic grimace and pointed at the cell in my hand. "I may be awhile."

"Perhaps you'd like to join us at the party tonight?"

Him and his oh-so charming friends? "Party?"

"The grand opening celebration."

That party. The one I'd agreed to attend in exchange for a villa. "I'll be there. Maybe we'll run into each other."

A flash of annoyance darkened his features but he nodded and sauntered back to his friends.

"Who were you talking to?" Mia demanded.

"No one."

"No one has a voice?"

"Some guy was hitting on me," I whispered. "He left."

"Then why are you whispering?"

"It's hard to explain."

"What are you doing down there, Poppy?"

"Like I said, I need time away." Then, because I didn't know how to quit when I was ahead, I added, "There are no memories here."

"They give you a villa?"

"Yes." A splash of uh-oh washed down my spine. "Why?"

"How many bedrooms?"

Uh-oh.

"I'm coming down there."

"You don't have to, Mia."

"I wanna come!"

"I want to be alone."

"Then you can be alone with me."

"Mia." Arguing with her was like arguing with a brick wall, but harder and less rewarding.

"I'll see you tomorrow."

"Mia—" exasperation curled my fingers.

"I'm coming. You can thank me later." With that, she hung up.

I stared at the cell in my hand.

Laughter had resumed down the length of the pool deck and I glanced toward the group. They'd returned to their tequila shots. Except for Javier and the man who'd stolen Marta's top—they were both staring at me.

Their gazes managed to be both hot and cold

I shivered and threw my things in my pool bag. I'd be safer away from bellies, mustaches, tattoos, scars, and tequila shots.

ALSO BY JULIE MULHERN

The Country Club Murders

The Deep End

Guaranteed to Bleed

Clouds in My Coffee

Send in the Clowns

Watching the Detectives

Cold as Ice

Shadow Dancing

Back Stabbers

Telephone Line

Stayin' Alive

Killer Queen

Night Moves

Lyin' Eyes

Big Shot

Fire and Rain

Killing Me Softly

Back in Black

Tight Rope

Bad Blood

Freddie Archer Series

Murder in Manhattan

ALSO BY JULIE MULHERN

www.ingramcontent.com/pod-product-compliance
Lightning Source LLC
LaVergne TN
LVHW010949070725
815504LV00012B/903